Redemption of a Wolf

(Red Dead Mayhem, Book 4)

T. S. JOYCE

Redemption of a Wolf

ISBN-13: 978-1726135306
ISBN-10: 1726135306
Copyright © 2018, T. S. Joyce
First electronic publication: August 2018

T. S. Joyce
www.tsjoyce.com

All Rights Are Reserved. No part of this book may be used or reproduced in any manner whatsoever without written permission, except in the case of brief quotations embodied in critical articles and reviews. The unauthorized reproduction or distribution of this copyrighted work is illegal. No part of this book may be scanned, uploaded or distributed via the Internet or any other means, electronic or print, without the author's permission.

NOTE FROM THE AUTHOR:

This book is a work of fiction. The names, characters, places, and incidents are products of the writer's imagination or have been used fictitiously and are not to be construed as real. Any resemblance to persons, living or dead, actual events, locale or organizations is entirely coincidental. The author does not have any control over and does not assume any responsibility for third-party websites or their content.

Published in the United States of America

First digital publication: August 2018
First print publication: August 2018

Editing: Corinne DeMaagd
Cover Photography: Wander Aguiar
Cover Model: Jase Dean

DEDICATION

For you.
You're reading this and that's so cool to me.
I'm your biggest fan.

ACKNOWLEDGMENTS

I couldn't write these books without some amazing people behind me. A huge thanks to Corinne DeMaagd, for helping me to polish my books, and for being an amazing and supportive friend. Looking back on our journey here, it makes me smile so big. You are an incredible teammate, C!

Thanks to Jase Dean, the cover model for this book. And thank you to Wander Aguiar and his amazing team for this shot for the cover. You always get the perfect image for what I'm needing.

And last but never least, thank you, awesome reader. You have done more for me and my stories than I can even explain on this teeny page. You found my books, and ran with them, and every share, review, and comment makes release days so incredibly special to me.

1010 is magic and so are you.

ONE

Something smelled good.

Kade lifted his chin and inhaled. Just over the scent of gasoline and oil, motorcycle exhaust and sweat...there was something clean.

He scanned the parking lot of the Harley Davidson store, but there were only small clusters of bikers in leather cuts tossing him suspicious glances. The Wulfe Clan was here and, hell yeah, he was ready to crack some werewolf skulls. He and that Clan of hot-heads had been going back and forth for months. They were the only shifters in this town he could depend on losing their heads and fighting him.

The newly sewn Blackwood Crow patch on his cut and the Lone Wolf symbol on his back confused the predators around here, but fuck it. He'd always confused people. That was the benefit to insanity—he kept everyone on their toes.

He sniffed again. The scent was so strong. He'd come here to pick a fight to satisfy the snarling monster in his middle, but the wolf was quiet now. Curious.

Find her.

"Shut up," he murmured. The last thing he needed was his wolf pushing him to eat someone. Again.

Fruit shampoo. Mango? No perfume, no body spray…just smelled like shampoo and pheromones. There was a female here who was close to her heat. Did humans go into heat? Hmmmm.

With his thick-soled riding boot, he kicked down the stand to his Fat Boy and settled the big motorcycle. He got off smoothly and gave the Wulfe Clan bikers a predatory smile as he passed right through the middle of them.

They were who he'd been hunting, his knuckles itching to blast some teeth, but they were safe from him for the moment.

They'd been making threats toward Red Dead Mayhem lately. Now…he didn't give a single shit about Clan politics, but he had an important interest in Red Dead Mayhem. His stepbrother Rike was Second there. And Rike's mate, Bailey, used to be part of the Wulfe Clan. She was shunned now for being with Rike, but Kade was...protective. Yeah, protective was a good, non-psychotic word for what he felt toward his stepbrothers and their mates, but possessive and territorial were more accurate. They didn't see him as family. They didn't know him or accept him, but he didn't care. They were his family to protect, so he would sit here on the outside for his whole life, letting his wolf have anyone who threatened them.

Rike and Ethan were safer than they even realized.

"Are we gonna have a problem today?" Darius, the Alpha of the Wulfe Clan, called after him as Kade opened the door to the store.

"I haven't decided yet," he answered. "Probably."

Right now, his wolf was on the hunt. Usually when he hunted, it was to kill, but this time, he wanted to pin a female against the dressing room stall and make her come over and over. That would keep the animal happy for an hour or two.

He stepped into the cavernous store, lined with rows of Harley bikes, clothes along the walls, riding helmets, leather jackets, motorcycle parts in the back...but none of that mattered. He saw her right away, looking at a used Harley Sportster Superlow in a metallic maroon. She had blond hair that she'd ironed straight and pulled into a high ponytail. She wore sunglasses inside. Hmmm. Her skin was fair, as though she didn't spend much time outside, and her profile was interesting—long, straight nose, thin lips, jawline that could cut glass. A black tank top hugged a fit physic and good boobs. Probably a B-cup. Small and perky. A handful. A pair of skinny jeans showed off the curves of her round ass. On her feet were a pair of shit-kicker riding boots. No wedding ring on her finger. He sniffed again. She'd filled the entire room with her scent. Smelled ready for sex. Ripe. He stifled a groan and adjusted his swelling dick. She was going to feel so good pulsing around him.

Maybe he should tell her his name beforehand so she could scream it.

She slid her slender leg over the seat and settled onto the motorcycle with her back to him. *Mmmm, tempting little temptress. Never give your back to a predator, woman.*

He sauntered toward her.

A salesman made a beeline for him, but Kade snarled "fuck off" before the salesman could get out a "Can I help you?"

He wound through the maze of Harleys up front, and when he was two rows of bikes away from the sweet little cupcake he was about to devour, he parted his lips to wow her with a one-liner that would make her ovaries beg for him.

"Stop right there, Wolf," the woman demanded without turning around.

Kade startled to a stop. "What?"

"I said fuck off." She gave an empty smile over her shoulder and lifted her delicately arched eyebrows. "Like you told that sales person."

Interesting. She heard him from that long distance. One good sniff, and he could tell why. She smelled like fruit shampoo, pheromones, and fur. Shifter.

Well...this was unfortunate. From his experience, female shifters tended to be battle axes from a life of hanging with dominant shifters.

Because of the animal inside her, she was

practically wearing a chastity belt made of fire and teeth. Fuck.

"It's your lucky day," he said low as he made his way to the motorcycle next to hers. Another Sportster and too small for his likes, but the seat was comfortable enough, and it was leaning heavy on a kickstand that angled him right toward her.

"Disagree," she muttered, gripping the handles of the motorcycle she was balancing. "First, I'm in heat, which sucks. Second, I had to make my way through an entire Clan of werewolves outside. And now, one of you little dorks followed me inside. No four-leaf clovers here. Seriously, fuck off."

Kade let off a surprised laugh. "No one has ever called me a little dork before. I meant it's your lucky day because I'm not attracted to female shifters at all. You're instantly safe from my advances, though I have to tell you, I would've given you some serious relief from those heat pangs you're going through. I could've kept up with your needs. No strings attached, condoms every time, no little baby bear or fox or... What are you?"

The woman took off her sunglasses and hooked them into the cleavage of that sexy tank top, and then she leveled him with eyes so bright green he pulled the motorcycle off the kickstand and angled away just to put a few more inches between them. "You look creepy as shit."

"Yeah, well so do you. Your eyes are almost white. Go back to your Clan."

"My Clan ain't here."

The girl frowned. "Lie."

"I'm not a liar. You could ask me anything, and I would answer. I have no shame and no agenda."

"Why did you approach me?"

"You smell good and I wanted to fuck."

Her frown deepened before her gaze flickered to the Blackwood Crow patch on his left pec, right above his name patch. "Kade," she murmured.

"You could've been screaming that name in the dressing room. I had plans. You ruined them with your shifterness."

The girl let off a soft laugh. It was pretty, like the dinging of a bell. Cute for a...whatever she was.

"Are you a predator shifter?" he asked.

"Yes."

"Ew."

She laughed again and shook her head, stared at

the gauges on the motorcycle. "You'll really answer any question I ask honestly?"

Kade shrugged. "Until it bores me."

"What is a wolf doing in the Blackwood Crow Clan?"

"Protecting the Alpha."

"Who is the Alpha?"

"Ethan Blackwood."

"Why would you pledge to that psycho?"

Kade smiled. "Because I'm a bigger psycho."

"No, really," she said softly. "I know Ethan. He's not okay. He shouldn't be anyone's Alpha. Why did you pledge?"

Kade considered the question. He looked down at the sportster between his thighs and thought about getting up and leaving. "I don't like talking to people much."

"And yet here you are," the girl said.

Fuck it. "Ethan is my brother."

The girl looked truly stunned. "Rike is his brother, and they're crow shifters. You're a wolf. You can't be his brother."

"And yet here I am," he murmured, using her words. "This is boring. Good luck in here, Predator

Female."

He stood to leave, but she said, "Mountain Lion."

Kade stopped his retreat and looked down at her. "You're safer from me with every word you say, woman. I like my females submissive."

She smiled up at him with canines too sharp. "Ew," she said, using his response from earlier. Huh. She was kind of interesting.

The girl looked back over her shoulder to the exit doors where the Wulfe Clan was still milling around outside. They had cold beers in their hands now. They would be here for a while.

"Can I ask you more questions?" she asked.

"No. I told you I'm bored."

"Not about your life, Wolf. About motorcycles."

He studied the one she was balanced on. "That one is a 2014 Sportster. The color is meh, but it looks good if kept up. And it's a good size for you. You look hot—"

"I do?" she asked quick.

Kade snorted. "Lady, you know what you look like. You don't need compliments from a little dork like me." He didn't mean to snarl at the end, and he shook his head hard to stop the noise.

"Are you messed up?" she asked low.

"Yes."

"Well...you're hot, too. I mean when you are on a motorcycle. I don't like wolves, so you're safe from me, too."

Hmm. She was just interesting enough for him to take a seat back on the black Sportster he'd been relaxing on a minute ago. "Why don't you like this one? It's a better color and is newer."

"This one is cheaper, and I like metallic red."

"Black is the best color for a Harley."

"That's your opinion. All the Harley's outside are black with black pipes. I want something different. When I walk out of my bar, I want to immediately know which one is mine."

"You have a bar?" he asked. "I like whiskey."

"All wolves do, don't they?"

"Stereotyping already?"

"Yep. That's all those assholes drink when they come in." She gestured toward the Wulfe Clan with the flick of her fingers. "And then they fight and break stuff and start shit with my Clan and the Two Claws Clan."

"Hmmm. What bar?"

"The GutShot."

"You own the GutShot? In Darby?"

"Me and my dad took it over when my first Clan fell."

Oh, he knew what had happened to her first Clan. The Darby Clan fell because they were stupid enough to go after the bear shifters in the Two Claws Clan. Obviously, survival instincts weren't strong with them.

"I thought no one in the Darby Clan survived," he murmured.

The girl wouldn't meet his eyes anymore, and there was sadness in her voice when she said, "Maybe no one did."

"You don't think you survived?"

"I didn't survive as I was. I'm not the same me anymore." She cleared her throat. "Is this a good buy or not? I've come to see it four times this week."

He wanted to observe her longer. Wanted to figure out how she did that—went from sad to stoic in a breath. Tough girl. She'd given him something just now. A peek into what made her tick. Little survivor probably reinvented herself completely to live through all those broken bonds and be okay.

A long snarl rattled his throat again, reminding him of why he couldn't be around nice things. The wolf was good for a fuck or two, a one-night stand, and then he messed everything up. As apparent by the deep frown the girl just gave him.

"If you've come to see it four times in a week, it feels special to you. On motorcycles, when you know, you know. Is this your first one?"

"Yeah. My car broke down, and it'll cost more to fix it than it's worth. I live near my bar. And since everything went to shit, I want to do something just for me. I'm always watching the MCs rippin' out of the bar on their Harleys and, lately, I've been wishing more and more I was riding one, too. My Alpha has one. So does my dad. I don't want to ride on the back."

"You mean you don't want to ride bitch?" he said with a baiting smile.

The woman rolled her eyes and turned on the Sportster. It roared to life.

"Well, now I'm liking it," he said over the engine noise.

"Why's that?"

"Whoever owned it before put good pipes on it.

People will hear you coming a mile away. Loud is best on a Harley. And I might not like the color, but it suits you. You ain't one of them little dorks outside."

"Ha!" She laughed loud. "No, I am not."

He leaned over and flipped the price tag toward him. "Fifteen thousand, my ass," he muttered. "Hey!" he called to the sales person he'd told to fuck off.

The salesman strode right on over with a big smile plastered to his face. "You finally deciding to pull the trigger?" he asked the girl.

"Uuuuh—" she stalled.

"Not for this price," Kade growled, not hiding his animal eyes at all. He pointed out the age, the mileage, the worn tires, the engine and what it was worth, and the scratches on the paint job that said this thing had hit concrete hard at some point. "Now, you and I both know this thing is worth maybe seven thousand, and you have it marked up to fifteen? That's bullshit. What's the best you can do on it?"

The salesman looked like a deer caught in headlights. "Let me talk to the sales manager and see."

"Seven grand, plus you take your cut for a couple thousand for title, tags, and profit, all that crap. Come back to us with an offer of nine-five max, and she'll walk out of here with it."

"That's an insane amount of money to take off a motorcycle," said the sales guy, Owen, his nametag read.

"Well, go back and look at your books again. You guys obviously mislabeled this price tag. No one on Earth or in Hell would ever buy this ride for that much. You know it and I know it. Go recalculate, Owen. Find the mistake. Re-label it or whatever you have to do, or this thing will sit on your showroom floor for months. And then you'll sell it at auction for a fraction of what this lady here is willing to pay."

"Trina," the girl murmured. "My name's Trina."

Hot name. Kade corrected himself, "For what Trina will pay."

Owen nodded and spun on his heel, jogged off toward the sales desk in back.

"Nine-five!" Kade called out. "Sell a motorcycle, Owen. Get that commission."

Trina was watching Owen talk to the sales manager in back with her jaw hanging down to her perky little tits. "Will they really consider nine-five?" she whispered.

"Nah. They'll come back with eleven, and then it's up to you to purchase it."

"It's way better than it was. I only haggled them down to fourteen thousand."

"Yeah, well, they really did make some mistakes when they marked this bike. Look at 'em." He jerked his head toward the pair of them frowning at a computer screen, looking stressed out. "Somebody fucked up, and they know it."

Fuck her from behind.

Kade shook his head and swallowed a snarl. His inner psychopath was making a not-so-rare appearance. He needed to Change and kill something. Sex with this little she-cat was off the table. He really didn't like other shifters, and he'd be good-goddammed if he stuck his dick in one. "All right, Trina, I'm off to find more trouble. Enjoy your heat."

He made his way out of the Harley store and, sure, he could feel her watching him leave, but that didn't change a thing. Shifter females were always on the hunt for a mate, not a hook-up, and he was built for one thing—being alone. It had always been like that for him. There were big reasons he hadn't pledged to a single Clan until his thirty-fifth year of life. He didn't play well with others. Friendship made his wolf all murdery and overprotective, so for the survival of people here in his territory, he stayed far away from meaningful relationships.

The tasty little cougar would've been fun to fuck…if she hadn't been a tasty little cougar. Shifters were off-limits to a monster like him.

But also…

He didn't like that Trina had trouble getting in the door because of the Wulfe Clan fuckin' with her. She was in heat and likely had been singing an unintentional siren song to these asshole's dicks.

So, he dug deep and found his chivalry. He would make it safe for her to leave.

The second he stepped outside, he made his way past the Clan, knocking two in the shoulder. He assured them, "We have a problem now."

The Alpha, Darius, laughed and asked, "Are you fuckin' serious, Lone Wolf? There's one of you and a dozen of us."

Huh. The prick was right.

So Kade pulled the rings off his fingers so it would be a fair fight.

TWO

He was beating the shit out of the entire Wulfe Clan.

Trina stood there plastered to the front window with her mouth hanging open. Who was this guy? She'd smelled him before she'd seen him. Definitely a dominant werewolf. She would know that scent of fur anywhere. The Wulfe Clan had been badgering her since she went into heat a few days ago, and he'd smelled just like the rest, only bigger. Or maybe he just felt bigger. And also sick. He felt off, like he was head-sick. His rapidly changing eye color from silver to blue and blue to silver backed up her instincts. He hadn't even hid his crazy eyes either. Just sat down, stared at her directly, and talked like they'd known each other for a year.

Hot guy for a werewolf. He had longer hair that hung down in his eyes, but short on the sides. He wore a leather cut and a black T-shirt, both of which he was currently removing, and hoooooolyyyyy shit, Lone Wolf was ripped. Not just a hard body, but hard like a metal statue of a body builder. Was that an eight-pack? She counted real quick before he spun away from her and blasted one of the Wulfe Clan across the jaw. That dude went down like a sack of dog shit, which was exactly how she'd seen every werewolf before now. This was awesome. He leveled two more. Trina laughed and looked around. Was anyone else seeing this? She could leave here with no problems by stepping over the bedraggled carcasses of an entire Clan. She should video this.

But when she aimed her phone, Owen cleared his throat behind her. "Eleven-two is the best we can do."

Oh, Lone Wolf was good. "Make it eleven, and I'll sign the paperwork and pay in cash right now."

"Deal," he said quickly. "Aw maaaan," he drawled, standing beside her and watching the fight. "Second time this week."

"That you know of," she murmured, grinning at

the Lone Wolf who was now on top of one of the remaining men, pummeling the life out of him. That man was a fighter, fast as fuck, and he didn't do the expected. As highlighted by him stopping mid-punch to reach out and yank the leg of a man who was charging him. The wolf went off balance and landed on his ass. Was Lone Wolf laughing? Yep, he was dribbling blood from a split lip and wearing the biggest grin, like he'd never had so much fun. Short scruff on his face, blindingly silver eyes, great smile if she ignored all the blood, and built like a Mack truck. He had tattoos down one arm and perfectly puckered man nipples. He had pecs etched like stone and strips of muscle over his hips that dove into his low-slung jeans and created a V-shape to his hotboy body.

Seriously, who was this guy?

Her cougar was practically panting. God, she needed to settle down. It was just her heat, that's all. If she wasn't in season, she wouldn't be lusting after a volatile werewolf. No way. She made better life decisions than that.

Ripping her gaze away from the fight actually took some effort.

"If you come this way, we can start on the

paperwork," Owen said.

"Sweet, I could use the dickstraction."

"Did you just say dickstraction?" Owen asked, walking beside her.

"Uh, no. I said dickstraction." Oh, hell. She cleared her throat and enunciated primly, "Distraction."

Leading her to the sales station at the back, Owen tossed a frown over his shoulder at the fight and shook his head. He gave her a pamphlet on the riding classes they offered and then introduced her to the finance manager, Garth.

By the end of all that, she was rushing to sign the last four pages. Why? Because her cougar was a little horn-ball who wanted to go see how the fight had ended up. She didn't know anything about that man other than his Clan, and she wasn't in a rush to track down Ethan Blackwood. All she wanted to do was thank the man for helping her haggle the price of the motorcycle. And for beating up the Wulfe Clan. And maybe silently thank his momma for makin' a man like him because, holy sheeyit, she was still thinking about his defined hip muscles. She bet he was really good at humping. Humping? *Good grief, girl, get a grip.*

After she finished up, the proud new owner of a Sportster Superlow, she rushed to the front window to find him long gone, along with the Clan. All that remained were small blood-puddles on the concrete. With a little sigh of disappointment, Trina made her way back to the gathering sales members. They rang a bell to signify her new life as a Harley owner.

Today had been different from the string of identical days over the last few months.

Today had been blood and wolves and confusion and Harleys.

Today had been a beautiful distraction from all the crap that had gone wrong in the last year.

Today had been excitement and a breath of fresh air, thanks to one mysterious werewolf.

Too bad he was crazy.

THREE

"No smoking!" Trina yelled as a local sauntered through the front door of the GutShot with a lit cigarette hanging out of his mouth.

"What? Since when?" he asked around the smoke-stick.

"Since the sign on the door said so." She set down the glass she was drying and jammed a finger at the No Smoking sign.

"What is this one?" he asked, gesturing to a sign with a logo of a pregnant squirrel standing on her hind legs, cradling her swollen belly.

"Well, that one was a bit much," Tenlee said with a sigh as she stretched her arms and stuck the swell of her belly out farther.

"It means there's pregnant shifters in here, and you'll have to smoke out on the porch," Trina demanded.

"A squirrel shifter gets more rights than me now?" the man asked rudely.

"Yep, and now I'm not serving you, so why don't you take your precious cigarette and fuck off to somewhere else."

"I've been coming here for years!"

"Don't care. Don't let the door hit you where the good lord split you, Bart."

"Trina," Tenlee murmured, "stop chasing off all the customers. Bart, come on in. The rules of the bar have just changed a little, but it's still the same old GutShot. I'll get you a glass of whiskey."

"Thank you," Bart said with a snort at Trina. "At least some shifters pretend to have manners."

Trina flipped him off and went back to drying glasses while Tenlee closed the cover of her math book and waddled around to the back of the bar top.

"Remind me again why trigonometry is so important," Tenlee grumbled.

"It's not. But you wanted your GED before the baby comes, so you get to muddle your way through that crap like the rest of us had to do."

"You're a grumpy little cuss when you're in heat."

"Need. Dick."

Tenlee laughed and poured Bart a glass of the cheapest whiskey The GutShot carried. "What about Kasey?"

"A crow shifter? No spanks."

"A human?"

"Nope, nope, nope. I would break them."

"Okay, Miss Picky, the big predator shifters around here are all paired up, and their ain't no unmated mountain lions left but you and your dad, so I'm out of suggestions."

A mentally unstable werewolf sounded like a good time in the sack, but she wasn't going to say that little gem out loud.

One week. It had been one week since she'd met Kade in the Harley Davidson store. A lot had happened since then. She'd taken her first riding class and ridden her new motorcycle to work every day. She'd slept seven times. She'd eaten twenty-five meals, watched three Netflix marathons, re-painted her bathroom, and had six work shifts at the GutShot. Basically, a week felt like an eternity. Add to that she couldn't get the crazy wolf off her mind, and she was still in heat. Yeah, nothing was okay. She was an emotional basket case. Blowing a flyaway piece of blond hair out of her face, she frowned at the clock and muttered, "Why is it so dead today?"

Bart the Fart raised two fingers and stopped sipping his whiskey long enough to suggest, "Because you offend all your customers with your bitchiness?"

"Drink your whiskey and stop getting on my damn nerves, Bart."

Bart pulled four one-dollar bills out of his back pocket and slapped them on the counter. "Each time you're rude, I'm taking away from your tip." He plucked the top dollar bill off the pile, arched his eyebrows, and shoved it back in his pocket.

Trina hated everyone and everything.

"It's probably because the Wulfe Clan comes in here on Fridays, and they're late," Tenlee suggested. "There's ten people in here buying. It just seems peaceful because there's no yelling and mauling and bleeding."

"Huh. You're right," Trina murmured. The Wulfe Clan did come in here at the same time every Friday. That was their tradition. They blew off steam after every work week. Now, she hated them and they were obnoxious, but they paid their tabs and kept her busy enough, so they were fine by her. Two more hours until the weekend rush, or it was sure to be a boring time if the Wulfe Clan didn't show.

At the sound of a Harley, she straightened up and looked out the back window to the gravel parking lot. It was a single Harley engine, and a silly part of her hoped it was him—Kade. She'd been keeping an eye out for him around town ever since she found out that Ethan had started up his Blackwood Crow Clan in Corvallis, not too far from Darby.

It was Darius Wulfe, the Alpha of the Wulfe Clan, parking out back, not Kade. And a few moments later, she heard the engines of the others in the Clan. They parked in a line, right next to her Sportster.

Okay. Okay, it wasn't the wolf she had hoped to see, but this was better. There was no chance of her cougar going ho and trying to bang one of these jerks in the ladies bathroom stall. Plus, this Clan drank like fish and actually paid for those drinks, so bonus bonus.

"Why do you look all disappointed?" Tenlee asked suspiciously from where she'd taken her seat at the bar top to study again. Her mouse-brown eyebrows were drawn down, and her soft brown eyes were all squinty and suspicious.

"I'm not!" Trina said. "I'm happy. I love...wolves. In my bar. Our bar. My bar and my dad's bar. Because money." *Dear goodness, stop talking!*

"Does being in heat make you horny *and* weird?" Tenlee asked.

Trina ignored her and began setting out shot glasses. The Clan always bought a round of whiskey shots the second they came in and, in general, werewolves were a predictable lot. Well...all but Kade.

Slamming his fist on the counter, Darius growled, "The usual." His eyes were too light green to pass for human but oh, well. Shifters were out, might as well own it. Trina didn't bother to cover up her eye color when she was working the bar either.

"How many you got comin' in tonight?" Trina asked.

"The fuck does it matter?" Darius rumbled, scanning the bar as his Clan took the bar stools around him.

"Uuuuh, so I know how many shots to pour, you

gigantic twat-waffle."

"What did you call me?" Darius snarled.

Trina sucked in air and made the words real clear and slow for the idiot. "Twaaat. Waff—eek!"

Tenlee yanked her back. "Shhhh!" she demanded, her eyes roiling with reprimand. "You shouldn't talk to an Alpha like that," she hissed.

"He ain't my Alpha." She pulled at the low neck of her tank top and fanned her face. "Is it hot in here?"

"It's the heat," one of the wolves she hadn't met before said.

"No shit, Sherlock," Trina muttered. "Of course I get hot in the heat."

"No, I mean your heat. It's making you run hotter."

"I'll say," rumbled another, a blond with dark eyebrows and silver eyes. It was Mick, Darius's Second. His nostrils flared as he inhaled. "Way hotter."

"Barf," Tenlee said. "How many shots do you want, pervs?" she asked as she eyed three more Clan filing past her to take seats at the bar.

"All of us plus two more," Darius said. "And since you're probably real dumb, I'll count it up for you.

Nine in all. Make them doubles. The whole Clan's here tonight." He gave a feral smile. "We're on the hunt."

"First off, Tenlee isn't dumb. And second..." Trina lifted a pair of scissors from the bar and made a quick *snip* sound as she closed them. "You aren't hunting me if you wanna keep your werewolf balls intact."

"God, you're a pill," Mick said, clutching his nuts protectively. "You're usually nice and just get us drinks."

Trina smiled brightly. "It must be the heat."

"You're the worst bartender in the world."

"Thank you," she muttered, pouring whiskey into a row of shot glasses.

"That wasn't a compliment."

"That'll be eight thousand dollars," she said, ignoring Tenlee's look of utter bafflement at her.

The wolves ignored her and made a toast. "To the hunt," Mick said.

Trina knew better than to ask what, or who, they were hunting. Those shifters closed up like little clams when they were sober. She just had to be patient, wait until they were a few drinks in, and then listen carefully for them to spill the beans. Which they did, but it took two doubles and a couple beers before Mick looked around and leaned closer to Darius. "He should've been here by now. This bitch should be drawing him in like a fly on a carcass. She reeks of pheromones, and he's dominant."

"So are you. Yet you're resisting her," Darius said low.

Trina moved a little farther away and knelt down in front of the ice machine with a clipboard, as if taking inventory. Of the ice cubes? Whatever, the wolves weren't paying attention.

"I'm resisting her because you laid down an order."

Whoo, it was getting hard to hear Mick, so Trina waddled backward a few steps, closer to the wolves.

"Because the longer she goes without being bred, the more desperate she will become. And so the more desperate he'll become to take her."

"Take who?" Tenlee asked, and now she sounded pissed. Uh oh, abort mission. The squirrel was a biter.

"Mind your own fuckin' business," one of the wolves, Gus, said in a growly voice. Oh, he must want to die today.

"I'll mind my own fuckin' business when you stop talking about girls like they're objects, loudly, in a bar full of shifters, ya dipshit." Uh oh, Ten was standing up now.

She was a buck-ten wet, about half the size of the smallest werewolf, but Mick scooted his chair loudly away from her anyway. Smart man.

"I know you aren't talking about using Trina as bait," Ten said loud enough for the entire bar to hear. "One, you couldn't put your dick in her if you tried because she has standards and doesn't fuck things that smell like wet dogs. You'll be keeping your little Vienna sausages to yourselves. Two, she's a motherfuckin' mountain lion. She ain't anyone's prey."

"Says the girl who helped destroy Trina's whole Clan of mountain lions," Darius growled, standing slowly.

"And who was it that survived all-out war?" Tenlee yelled. She jammed her finger at Trina. "I'll give you two fuckin guesses because you're super dumb, but you should only need one."

Oh, God, this was awesome. But also a little scary because Tenlee couldn't shift while she was pregnant, so it was really only Trina who had teeth and claws against the entire Wulfe Clan.

"'Scuse me," a local human called from down the bar. "I need another round."

"Be right there."

"Uh, now?" the man called. "You're just standing there."

"Ten," Trina drawled, "it's fine. The wolves aren't a threat—"

"Has everyone lost their minds?" Mick asked loudly. "Yeah, we're a threat. We're *werewolves*!"

"Cool. Do you get fleas?" the human asked, slurring slightly.

Mick stared at him with his mouth hanging open. "No!"

Trina pursed her lips against a smile because she shouldn't piss them off any more than they already were, but it was kinda funny.

"If you even knew…" Gus said, a rattling growl tainting his words. "If you even knew why we were here—"

"Gus, stop," Darius ordered, power infused in his words.

Gus's response was immediate. The words he'd been about to say seemed to choke him, and he stumbled forward, locked his arms against the counter like he was trying to stay upright. Ha ha, asshole. Kurt, Trina's Alpha and Ten's mate, would never put out an order like that for such a dumb reason.

"I think you should all leave," came a deep voice just loud enough to be heard across the bar.

Kade, the Lone Wolf, sat relaxed into a chair by the stage, one leg stretched out like he'd been there all night. He hadn't shaved his face in a few days, and the dark scruff on his chiseled jaw made his silver eyes look even brighter. He was looking right at Darius, unblinking. He was a very dominant wolf to stare down an Alpha like that. Or crazy. Or both. Dangerous combo. Hot combo. *What is wrong with you? Stop lusting after psychopaths.* Cute psychopaths. Trina purred really loud. *Oops.* Mick cast her a dirty look.

Fireworks were going off in her ovaries as Kade stood and stood and stood until he towered over the humans who had been talking in clusters around him.

"How the hell did he sneak in here?" Mick whispered. None of his Clan answered him. They all just stood slowly and faced the newcomer while Trina balanced on her tiptoes to try to see around them.

Damn them for blocking her view of the Adonis. Her hoo-ha needed her eyeballs to see him and report his growing hotness promptly. Oooooh, look how he walked. Grace and power and some shit-stomper boots that were definitely going to smash some faces if the murderous look on his face said anything.

"So the hunter becomes the hunted, huh?" Kade asked, coming to lean casually against the bar near the drunken human.

"Do *you* have fleas?" the man asked.

Kade gave a slow blink and a terrifying look to the man. "It's probably best you fuck off."

The man made an "eek" face and backed away slowly.

Trina was going to make Kade a drink. She was going to make him a drink and not charge him, then it would be like her buying him a drink and, basically, this would be a date. He didn't know it, but it was happening right now.

Refusing to serve him the same booze as she did for the other lesser peon werewolves, she pulled the best vodka out of the cabinet on the back wall and tiptoed over to stand by him.

"What are you doing?" he asked, frowning down at where she was pouring two drinks, one for him and one for her.

"Our first drinks," she whispered.

He sighed. "I have to fight these assholes first. Raincheck?"

"No! Because you disappear for a week at a time, and this might be my only chance to cheers you for getting me my motorcycle for way cheaper."

"You look hot riding it, by the way," he murmured, pulling one of the shots to him.

"You saw me riding it?"

"Oh, yeah. I watch you all the time. I'm a stalker like that."

"Hmmm," she said in a mushy voice. He liked her. She wished he was railing her from behind in the office in back right now. *Puuuuuuurrrrrrrr.*

"Horny little pussy, aren't you?" he asked with a devil-may-care smile that made her want to rub against his leg like an overgrown housecat.

"Mmmm hmmm."

"Hello!" Mick said, striding for Kade.

Kade tossed back the shot fast and leaned over the bar. Time slowed to a crawl. His lips crashed onto hers, and then he sat there, mouth against hers, sucking gently for a few moments before he was ripped backward. Mick had him, but Kade was smiling, and his eyes were almost white when he was pulled away from her. He didn't look worried at all, but Trina's senses came back with the force of an avalanche.

It was him versus the entire Wulfe Clan. Again.

"Where's your Clan?" she yelled.

"Don't have one tonight," he called as he blasted a fist against Mick's jaw. The wolf went flying. Shit, shit, shit, that was close to the window. Dad was already on the edge and would kill the next SOB who broke a window in this place!

Wait, didn't have a Clan? Yes, Kade did. He was a Blackwood Crow! Errr…Blackwood Wolf?

"Ten! Can you call—"

"Already on it," Ten called from over by the wall-phone. She was talking into the landline, but it wouldn't be quick enough. Kade had half a dozen guys on him now.

Another wolf went flying out of the pile.

"Don't break the windows!" she cried, rushing around the counter. "Aaah!" she screamed as the fight suddenly turned directions and Mick came flying at her. She couldn't get out of the way fast enough and slammed back against the bar top.

She shoved the man off her and snarled. There was no stopping the animal inside her now.

"Oh, shit!" Mick murmured through a split lip.

"Oh, shit" was right. With a moment of agonizing pain and popping of her bones, Trina went to all fours, and her mountain lion ripped out of her. She let off a panther scream just to worn those wolves what was coming for them.

She was completely fine with being Kade's Clan tonight.

****

Kade totally had this…until he heard the panther.

It was a cross between a roar and a scream, and it chilled his blood. He shoved one of the wolves off him hard and stood up straight so he could see where that blood-curdling death-promise came from. But that one moment of lost focus got him blasted across the jaw. Hoooooly shit that hurt! The guy was pummeling him now as he struggled to recover because half of him wanted to make sure the cougar, Trina, was all right. What the fuck were his instincts doing? *Protect yourself, man!*

Now there were three on him, and he couldn't see the animal, but he could hear the murmur of panicked voices and the growling of a predator. Trina smelled like heat and rage. Good gah, was it possible for her to get even hotter?

When a fist landed right on his shoulder blade, he grunted and pitched forward. Wait, was he going to lose this fight? Didn't matter how many assholes he fought at once, he'd never lost! Kade twisted and caught the wolf's fist, ground his bones to dust in his hand, and shoved him into the wall. Shit, he almost hit one of the front windows, and Trina had said not to break the windows.

Crash!

A crow with a circle of white feathers around his neck came flying through the window pane, and after him sailed a black wolf. Aw, mother fucker! There went Trina's one request.

Well, the cavalry had arrived. Like he needed help. Kade grunted under a blow and then spun, pummeled the guy's face a few times before he dropped like a sack of stones. Ethan, his stepbrother and Alpha was probably, he didn't know, pecking someone's eyes out like crows did, and he could see Leah clear as day, her black wolf ripping into the shoulder of that blond chode who had pulled him away from Trina's lips. Ha. She looked like she was gonna kill him. And by the bar, a massive, lethal mountain lion had her front claws wrapped around a guy who was screaming bloody murder as she sank her teeth into him. He Changed into a giant gray wolf, but Trina didn't back down a bit. The wolf bit into her and shook hard, but she slapped him with one powerful paw, and he went sprawling into a row of bar stools like she was bowling. Holy shit, this was awesome. Kade stood there looking from one shifter fight to another. He got blasted across the jaw by some short guy built like a tank, but he just laughed and spat blood onto the floor. Another wolf Changed, and inside of him, a snarl rattled his entire body. Uh oh.

He couldn't Change. Couldn't. No one in here would survive, Trina included. His wolf wasn't okay.

Kade backed toward the door just as two mottled brown wolves charged him. The snapping of his own bones sounded, and he hunched against the pain in his hands as the Change began. No, no, no!

The wolves leapt, and he gritted his teeth as he was thrown backward into the door. The barrier became nothing but splinters exploding around them.

There were red and blue lights blinding him, and sirens that hurt his ears, but it wasn't louder than the roaring of his animal in his head. Everything was overwhelming his senses. Everything hurt as he fought to slow the Change down. "Trina," he choked out to the gorgeous, sandy-colored cougar stalking out of the bar toward him. Her ears were flattened, and her lips were pulled away from long, curved canines in a hiss as she zeroed in one of the wolves Kade was fighting.

She hadn't seen his wolf yet though, and he didn't want her to. Not ever. "Trina, run," he choked out in the seconds before the monster tore out of him.

Pain burned through his neck where a cream-colored wolf, Darius, latched on and was shaking him. He didn't know where the other two were now, nor did he care. One wolf at a time. One death at a time. Kade went to work, and he wouldn't stop until there was only a pile of bodies left.

Boom! Boom! Boom!

Fire burned from stabbing pain at his ribs and

hind quarters. Someone was shooting him with something...needles? Fire, fire...fire. He couldn't breathe, couldn't think straight, and his body was going numb.

He fought as long as he could, put his teeth on that wolf as much as he could because he was determined to take him down with him...

The second he lost feeling in his paws, Kade hit the ground hard, his jaws still latched onto Darius's throat. The Alpha wasn't dying fast enough...but if Kade could just hold on...

But as the wolf drew a a long, ragged breath, Kade's body seized...and he died first.

FOUR

Trina's head was killing her. Must've been the tranquilizers that were giving her one gnarly hangover. She buried her face in her hands and squeezed her eyes tightly closed, but that didn't help the stabbing pain behind her eyes. Not even a little.

Animal control had apparently been training the cops in Darby, but she was pretty sure they'd damn near overdosed Kade with those tranquilizers.

In the cell beside her, which was really a metal-barred cage underneath the precinct, lay a massive gray and white wolf. He was facing away from her and lying in a crimson puddle on the concrete floor of his cage. She checked to make sure he was breathing every few seconds. She wanted to kill whoever shot him with three tranqs. But then, maybe that's what it took for a shifter like him. Kade had still damn near killed that other wolf, even drugged up. She'd never seen anything like him. He was the definition of power and violence. Of bloodlust. His silver eyes had gone empty the second after he'd told her to run.

Kade really was crazy.

Being a rogue did that to some animals, especially dominants.

And Kade was a beast. The wolf he'd been fighting was none other than Darius Wulfe, Alpha of the Wulfe Clan. And Kade had bested him. If he had wanted to take the Clan, he'd won that right tonight with almost no effort.

She'd never seen a monster like Kade, and that was saying something. Her New Darby Clan was allied with the Two Claws Clan, and they were bear shifters with very little control.

Another breath. Thank God.

"What happened?" Ethan Blackwood said in a raspy voice from the cell on the other side of her.

His long hair on top was mussed, and he was on hands and knees, his fists clenched on the concrete as he swayed. Beside him, a very naked Leah stretched and said, "Good morniiiiing," like she was in a bed and breakfast instead of jail.

Another breath from Kade. Thank God.

"Morning," she said to Leah, wincing as the volume of her own voice made her head hurt worse.

Leah stopped stroking Ethan's full beard long enough to look over at Trina and smile. "Are we in prison?"

"We're under the Darby Precinct in the shifter containment room—"

"Owooooooo," came a muffled howl through the walls.

"Or," she corrected herself, "*one* of the shifter containment rooms." She frowned at the closed metal door on the other side of the room. Apparently, the Darby Police Department had been expanding their shifter retention area. How many of the Wulfe Clan had they arrested? She couldn't remember in the chaos who got tranquilized. She hadn't been able to take her eyes off Kade until she'd blacked out.

"Babe!" Leah exclaimed, sitting up straight with a smile bright enough to light up the whole room. "I'm an official outlaw now! I'm a rebel! I have a rap sheet!"

Ethan drawled, "It's equivalent to spending a night in the drunk tank but—"

"It counts! I'm bad to the bone now," Leah murmured. "I need leather pants, and a tattoo."

Ethan snorted and pulled her close, hugged her up tight. "Woman, what am I gonna do with you?"

"Reverse cowboy?"

Oh God, Trina's head hurt even worse now. "Okay, well you two are gross," Trina murmured, rubbing her forehead. "There is a pile of clothes over there." She gestured to her own orange jumpsuit. "Not the most fashionable, but it'll hide your nethers."

"Why would we hide those?" Leah asked. "Being a nudist is the best part of being a shifter."

Ethan was chuckling now. It was weird seeing such a stoic man look…happy. While in jail. Outlaws were some crazy motherfuckers.

Another breath. Thank God.

"You should probably move away from the bars," Ethan warned her as he made his way to the neatly folded garments by his cell door.

Trina was leaning her face against the cold metal, watching Kade's wolf. "Why?"

"Because he's hunting you."

"What do you mean?"

"I mean he ain't asleep anymore. Move!" Ethan yelled, his voice echoing through the dim room.

Trina gasped as Kade's wolf flew into motion and charged her bars. She scooted out of the way just as his muzzle made it through and one of his canines left the faintest scratch on her arm.

Crab crawling backward, Trina didn't stop until her shoulder blades hit the cell bars that connected her cage to Ethan and Leah's. On the other side of the cage, Kade was going insane, eyes almost white and empty, gnashing his sharp teeth, his snarls filling the basement space, his dominance permeating every air molecule until it became hard to drag in a breath.

Panting in horror, she asked Ethan, "What's wrong with him?"

"He's a killer," the new Alpha of the Blackwood Crow Clan answered simply.

"But...he kissed me," she murmured, feeling slapped by the hatred in his eyes.

"Kade the man might have kissed you," Leah said. "But the wolf doesn't have feelings for anyone. He has one focus, and that's it."

"And what is that?" she asked, already knowing

the answer.

"To kill." Leah's voice echoed with sadness.

"Is he your maker?" Trina asked, turning to look at the silver-eyed girl. Her eye color matched Kade's.

"Not on purpose," Leah said with the ghost of a smile.

"What do you mean?"

"I mean Ethan ordered him to Change me when I was hurt, but it wasn't his wolf's choice. He wanted to kill me instead. He tried, but Ethan kept him off me." Leah inhaled deeply and brightened her smile. "But no one is perfect, and his wolf is just a quirk to deal with."

A quirk? Trina was looking at quite possibly the most dangerous shifter in existence. Why? Because a man who was out of control of his demons couldn't keep anyone safe. In the other cage, his wolf hadn't settled down at all. She'd never seen one so big in all her life. He had thirty pounds on the biggest Wulfe Clan wolf. His fur was dark gray with light points, but he was matted with blood. His hackles were raised down his back like some wild boar ready to charge. He was creating a soundtrack of terror from his growling and wolfish promises of destruction. Of pain.

She stared down at the faint scratch from where his bite had barely missed her forearm. If these metal bars weren't between them, would he stop himself from hurting her?

He glared at her with white-hot rage simmering in his eyes, his teeth bared. She'd fought the Wulfe Clan alongside him, but he still didn't feel any loyalty to her. He would still kill her if given the chance.

Bad wolf.

Big. Bad. Wolf.

FIVE

The sound of footsteps was barely audible over the constant sound of Kade's growling. It had been hours since she'd woken up down here, but there was still no word from the officers talking in a low murmur upstairs. Twice, one named Officer Donovan had come downstairs and gone straight into the room they were holding the Wulfe Clan, but he hadn't even bothered to look over at their cages.

And Kade's growling was only punctuated when he took a breath or snapped of his teeth if she moved even an inch.

Leah was a chatterbox. Trina liked her. She was funny and read like an open book. She practically hummed with happiness, and Ethan seemed to be feeding from his mate's natural joy. Seeing a big, badass crow shifter smile so much was a little weird, but it was good.

They'd told her how their Clan had formed and talked a little about Kade, but it was hard to focus with his attention pinpointed on her.

It made her sad.

Her animal had been so interested in him. She still was, just sitting inside her, watching him, always watching him…but she could never have him. No one could. He wasn't a safe bet.

Officer Donavan came stomping down. "Ethan and Leah, you're free to go." He lowered his voice as he unlocked their cell and muttered, "Rike and the entire damn Red Dead Mayhem Clan bailed you out."

"What about them," Ethan asked, gesturing to Trina and Kade.

"The New Darby Clan is working on her release, but what do you suggest I do with that one?" Officer Donavan asked, jerking his head toward Kade. "I can't just release him to the masses. He looks like he wants to kill you, and you're his own damn people. We will release him when he Changes back."

"That could take him days," Leah said. "He isn't

like other shifters."

"Clearly," Donovan said, resting his hands on his hips. "He stays until we deem him fit to be in public again." He frowned at the snarling wolf. "Just a heads up," he said low, "there's talk upstairs about him."

"What do you mean?" Ethan asked.

"I mean look at him. Can you blame the people in this town for wanting him gone? Or locked up? This isn't a threat. I'm actually rooting for you guys. This is me saying figure something out. Fix him."

"He isn't broken," Ethan gritted out through clenched teeth. "He's just different."

"You and I both know that's bullshit, man."

"Ethan," Leah whispered. "We can't leave him like this."

The look that passed between them was unreadable. But Ethan turned slowly to Kade and demanded in a booming voice, "Change back. Now."

A whine interrupted the snarling, and then Kade just...broke. That was the only word that came to mind as Trina watched his body shatter inward, bones snapping, muscles stretching, his face twisting with pain just before he Changed back to his human skin. Curled in on himself, Kade laid there panting.

Donovan looked equal parts disgusted and sympathetic. "We still have to keep him for observation for a while. I'll give you a call when he's ready for release."

Fury took Ethan's face and, for a moment, Trina thought he was going to smudge Donovan out of existence, take his keys, and set them both free, but Leah slipped her hand into his and whispered his name. Ethan relaxed immediately. Oh, his face was still seven shades of terrifying, but he looked a little less murdery. Ten points for Leah the Monster Tamer.

"We'll be outside when you're released," Ethan rumbled, his pitch-black eyes freezing Trina into place.

"O-okay."

Ethan and Leah followed Officer Donovan upstairs, and the echoing of those fading footsteps was a truly lonely sound.

Now it was just her and the crazy werewolf down here.

"Are you okay?" Kade sounded like he hadn't spoken in a week for how gritty his voice was.

His back was to her, so she could see the full

extent of his injuries from the fight. She had some too, but not like his. He had bite and claw marks all over him.

"I'm doing better than you," she murmured softly.

With a grunt, he pushed himself up, stood stiffly, and made his way to the pair of jeans someone had wadded up in the corner of his cell.

"No fair," she teased as he pulled them onto his powerful legs slowly. "All I got was this prison jumpsuit."

He slid a silver-eyed glance at her and gave the slightest smile. "How do you look pretty in every color?"

Stunned by his surprise compliment, she covered her shy smile by looking down at her pumpkin-orange outfit. It really was hideous though, so she huffed a laugh and said, "Well, apparently, you're still crazy."

He grunted and nodded once as he buttoned up the jeans. They fit him perfectly. Maybe those were his jeans someone had brought from the bar. They sat low on his hips, and as he fastened the belt, his eight-pack abs flexed. That man was fine. Terrifying, but fine.

Every movement he made looked painful. "Is that the first time you've had a forced Change?" she asked.

"Yep, and I'm probably gonna kill Ethan later for doing that. Fuckin' Alphas. That right there is why I miss being rogue."

"Being rogue is probably what made you like this."

"Like what?" he asked, eyes flashing.

"Crazy."

He huffed a breath and made his way to the other side of the cage. Now they were both sitting as far away from each other as possible. He slid down the bars, sat on the cement, and rested his elbows on his bent knees, staring off with a faraway look.

It was a long time before he spoke. "I wasn't always rogue."

They'd sat for so long in silence his admission surprised her. "What?"

He scooted a few feet closer to her cell, then cleared his throat and repeated, "I wasn't always rogue."

"Were you part of the Wulfe Clan? Is that why you have a beef with them?"

He rolled his head back and forth against a bar.

"My real mom is a wolf. High ranking. She's in the Wintercast Clan."

"Wow," Trina murmured, scooting a few feet closer as a reward to him for sharing with her. "I don't follow wolf Clans, but even I've heard of that one."

"Biggest wolf Clan in the world. Forty-two members last I heard, and my Mom is Second. And not mated either. She fought her way there. Highest ranking female of our kind."

"Why aren't you with her?"

"Because she's a piece of shit." When a snarl rattled his throat, he shook his head hard. The noise stopped.

"My dad is a beast. His wolf is as big as mine, and she picked him because she liked power. She pushed him into fights. Into Alpha Challenges. Back to back to back to back. I remember being six, maybe seven, and watching him fight every week. Fight, recover, fight, recover. He was always bleeding. Even when his wolf started getting addicted to the bloodlust, she didn't care. All she wanted was for her mate to be king. And when he lost a fight to the Alpha, she shamed him in front of the entire Clan. Alienated him. Made him look worthless when she should've had his back instead. He nearly died, and I remember sitting on the stairs in our house, holding onto the railing, so worried about my dad living, watching him struggle for each breath. His arm was hanging off the couch, just…dripping blood. It wouldn't stop. There was this huge puddle, and my mom was staring down at him with a look of …disgust. I tried to take care of him, but my Mom wouldn't allow me in the living room. I remember her face when she told me, 'He doesn't deserve your care. He would've been better off dying in that fight.' The next week, when my dad was well enough, he packed his suitcase and mine, and we left. My mom watched us leave like she didn't have any feelings for us at all. When we left, she told my dad, 'Don't want no pup that's as weak as you.' And that was that. She never called, never wrote a birthday card, nothing."

"Oh my gosh," she murmured. "No wonder you didn't want to be part of a Clan."

"You'll meet my dad."

"What?"

He rolled his head on the bars and gave her a sad smile. "I want you to meet him. He's who I wish I could've turned out to be."

When Trina scooted a few feet closer, he watched her with a curious frown, and then he scooted closer to her cell, too.

"What happened after you left the Wintercast Clan?"

A faraway smile transformed his face. "We got an hour down the road, and my dad got this old, ratty map out of the glove box of his Chevelle. He slapped it on the hood, and I'll never forget. It was hot, and we were out there sweatin' in the sun. I mean hot, like the hurts-your-lungs-to-breathe kind of hot. And he told me to close my eyes and pick a spot on the map. I did, and we drove a couple states over and landed in Stevensville, Montana."

"That's close to here."

"Yep."

"You stayed all this time?"

A nod. "My dad said we needed to put down good, strong roots because his wolf was half crazy from all the fighting and from being shunned from a Clan. You were right. Being rogue is hard on an animal. For a long time, it was just me and him, total boy's club, and then he met a quiet lady. A human. But she knew all about shifters because she'd been mated to one and had two crow boys. She'd lost them like my mom had lost me, but she was different. She was deeply hurt over their dad taking them. The kind of hurt that some women can't recover from. When they met, she was half-crazy too, just like my dad. She was hurting from grief—the kind that brings people to their knees. But in that first year they were together, I got to watch them fix each other. That lady included me in everything she did. I was growing into a monster with a wolf that would never be in control, but she loved me like her own flesh and blood boy anyway."

"Ethan and Rike's mom?"

"Yep."

Trina scooted all the way over and leaned her shoulder against the bars. "And that's why you pledged fealty to Ethan as your Alpha?"

For a few moments, Kade sat there, arms draped over his bent knees, rubbing his thumbnail absently with his other hand. But then he scooted over and rested on the bars beside her. "At first I was so jealous of Ethan and Rike. Their mother never stopped loving them or thinking about them for even a minute. And I knew my mom wasn't thinking of me at all. I thought I'd done something wrong. I couldn't understand how they had gotten a mother to love them. I couldn't figure it out. But one day, she asked me to go ride with her a few towns over on an errand. I was maybe eighteen at the time. Angry. Always angry. She took me to a post office with a big picture window up front. She sat next to me on a bench inside where we could see the hamburger joint across the street. I was sitting there, stomach growling, thinking about asking her if I could go get us a couple burgers, when two boys my age sauntered up to the front door. She sat up straight as if she'd been electrified. Her eyes filled with tears, and she didn't relax back in her seat until they'd finished eating and rode away on these old beater Harleys. I knew who they were from the tears in her eyes, but I asked anyways. She told me they were her boys, but one didn't remember his life with her, and the other was protecting him and didn't want to come around her because she reminded him of bad stuff that had happened to him." Kade swallowed hard and dropped his gaze to the floor in front of him.

Trina wanted to cry for him. This must've been very hard for a man like him to share. So she reached through the bars and squeezed his hand. When she moved to pull away, he flipped his hand over and squeezed hers back, then held it.

"After they left, she wrapped her arm around my shoulder and said, 'I love you like I love them. As far as I'm concerned, you're my boy. And those are your brothers.' So from then on, we went to that post office every Thursday because Ethan and Rike ate there every week at the same time. When they stopped that tradition, I started following them to find other places my mom could see them because she wasn't so sad when she got to see her other sons every week. And I taught myself how to watch them without getting caught."

"They never saw you?"

Kade shocked her and pulled her knuckles up to his cheek, rubbed his rough whiskers against her skin there as he smiled. "They saw me plenty. They just never realized it. I would sit near them at the bar or walk past them in restaurants, anything to be close to my brothers without messing with the balance my mom said was important for them to be okay. I had to. Being around them was something I needed to feel close to them—my brothers who didn't even know me. It taught me how to become invisible."

"When did you finally meet them?"

Kade shrugged up a shoulder. "A few months back, my mom told me she wanted me to come home for dinner, and they walked in. I was in shock. They didn't see me at first because I didn't want them to. I just wanted to watch how they were with Mom. She was having a big moment with all of us there in the same room. When they saw me, and my mom and dad told them I was family, my heart was pounding out of my chest. I was trying to keep cool, but I'd watched them for so long, and then suddenly they were talking to me. I fucked it up. The wolf came out, and I didn't get to stay for dinner. I had to go out the back door. So...the second I saw a chance to be in Ethan's Clan, I took it. I thought maybe if he sees me all the time, he could help make me a better man. Like him. Because he was a total monster, like me, but he's okay now. And sometimes I get dumb enough to think I can have that, too."

"You can," Trina said, intertwining her fingers with his. "If you want to, you can."

He huffed a breath and pressed his lips against her hand, and then gently, he put her hand back through the bars and settled it onto her lap before he slid away from her. "You saw my wolf. He will never change."

"Kade?" she murmured.

"Mmm?"

"I was wrong."

"About what?"

She swallowed hard. She wished he was still close to the bars so she could reach through and touch him again. "You aren't crazy at all."

SIX

Kade couldn't keep his eyes off her.

Trina blew a wavy strand of blond hair out from in front of her face and leaned onto the bar top. This was the best time of day to watch her because the sun was just going down and the lights inside Trina's bar, The GutShot, lit her up just right.

You aren't crazy at all.

She wore the cutest little frown, her lips pursed slightly, her blond eyebrows furrowed as she stared at a clipboard. It was inventory night. She always scrunched up her face like that when she was doing math.

You aren't crazy at all.

And yet here he was, sitting on a stack of crates

across the street, watching a girl who didn't know she was being watched. The prettiest girl he'd ever seen. She'd been doing up her make-up more lately. A wicked part of him hoped she was doing it for him. Her boobs pressed against a white tank top, and she was wearing his favorite jeans—the ones with the sparkles on the back pockets. He only got to see her ass when she came out from behind the bar to serve customers.

It would get rowdy soon, but this was the calm before the storm, the witching hour when he got to watch her all calm and collected. She smiled more when it wasn't busy. Sometimes he couldn't watch her at all if she was rushing around, trying to be enough for everyone in the bar. When she got stressed out, his wolf got stressed out, and that was a dangerous game.

It was also a new game.

It was the first time his animal had been anything but a mindless killing machine. Now…sometimes…he wanted to be a mindless killing machine for Trina.

You aren't crazy at all.

"Caw, caw, caw, caw!" a crow cried from the branches right above Kade's spying place.

He startled hard and snarled up at the massive black bird with the ring of white around his neck.

Ethan spread his wings and dove from the tree, and just before he hit the ground, he Changed and landed on his feet.

Kade glared at him. It was obnoxious that his Changes were so easy and controlled. "I can see your dick," Kade muttered, giving his attention back to Trina. "Fuck off."

"Ma told me how you used to help her watch out for us."

"So?"

"So...I'm keeping you company while you watch Trina tonight."

Kade tossed him a dirty look. "Don't need company. I'm fine on my own."

"Dude, you were the one who made us a Clan and decided I was supposed to be the Alpha."

"Shhh."

"And Leah said I should try to make us all closer."

"Ethan, shutthefuckup!"

"She also called the stars 'the glitter of the sky' and has been trying to convince me the man on the moon is actually a manta ray in the moon, and—"

"I'm literally going to murder you and not feel even one percent bad about it if you don't leave me alone," Kade whispered. "I'm busy. And good God, cover your balls up, man. You're making this weird."

Ethan had his hands on his hips and looked down at his dick with a frown. With an eye-roll, he covered up his junk and whispered, "Just so you know, it's already weird. Why don't you just go talk to her?"

"Because she deserves better."

"Horseshit. Let her decide that."

"I tried to eat her the other day in jail."

Ethan snorted and leaned on the tree trunk beside him. "Well, there's a word combination I never thought I would hear."

"Don't you have a mate to bone?"

"Nah, she's crafting tonight."

"Mod Podge Mondays," they both murmured in unison.

Kade kept the smile off his face, but just barely. As far as living creatures went, Leah was less annoying than most. But seriously, if he had to stand here with Ethan and his stupid balls out anymore, he was going to kill something. "Dude," he growled.

"Oh, right." Ethan covered himself up again. "So,

do you want the dirt on Trina or not?"

"Fuck. Off."

"'Cause I found her story pretty interesting when I was asking around town."

Kade narrowed his eyes at Ethan. His stepbrother had picked the perfect chum bait for a psychotic little shark like Kade.

"I think you'll find it interesting toooooo," Ethan sang low.

Kade could probably break both of Ethan's shin bones before he would even react. He considered it for a few seconds, but he would save his violence in case the Wulfe Clan came back in tonight and messed with his girl. *The* girl. Eh-hem. That girl over in the bar who was attached to no one. Fuck. Snarl. *Shut up, Wolf.*

You aren't crazy at all. In his head, Trina's voice sounded so pretty.

"Tell me," Kade gritted out, "and then fuck off."

"Trina Luna Chapman, born April tenth, nineteen eighty-three—"

"Ethan, I swear to you on everything that is holy—"

"Born and raised here, mom passed away when

she was seven, and she was raised by her dad, Cooper. That's the old codger coming out of the back office." Ethan gestured to the silver-haired man making his way toward a distracted-looking Trina. "Trina was born a shifter."

"What? I thought mountain lions were one of the shifters who could only have boys."

"Me, too, but apparently not. We have a party pack of weird shifters in this town," Ethan murmured. "We got a squirrel shifter Origin, the first of her kind ever, a natural born female moose shifter—"

"They're called cows—"

"Ha, if you met her on a bad day, you would *not* want to call her that. Vina damn-near killed me with her stompy, big-ass hooves. Anyway, then we have Trina, another female shifter, not Turned, born with the animal. So you know she's already tough as leather because girls have a hard time controlling predator animals."

"Leah doesn't," he pointed out.

Ethan chuckled. "I don't think anything ever stood a chance at getting Leah down. I thought for sure her wolf would be a psychopath, because look at her maker?" Ethan gestured to Kade. "But nope, her wolf is the happiest, most playful monster on the planet."

"Please," Kade muttered. "I saw her the other night in that bar fight. She's a killer."

"When she wants to be. When her people are threatened."

Kade wouldn't admit it out loud, but there was a little part of him that smiled because he was one of Leah's people. It was still new, being a part of a Clan, and Kade didn't really know how to navigate it quite yet.

In his head, he was still a lone wolf, but sometimes it was fun to pretend he wasn't.

Ethan looked around. "So, did you ride your motorcycle here? Or did you walk?"

Kade sighed and scooted farther away from Ethan. He could see Trina better from the shadows over here anyway.

"You still have your clothes on, so you didn't Change and run here—"

"Are you going to talk the entire time?"

"Well...probably."

Kade wanted to kick everything. "If you're going

to talk, talk about Trina."

The knowing grin that spread across Ethan's face was the most obnoxious thing Kade had ever witnessed, and he didn't even try to stop the snarl in his throat. Ethan was a crusty, obnoxious shrimp chode, and Kade was probably going to Change and eat him. He had two stepbrothers, so he could play that game twice. Right about now, he missed being an only child. He hadn't missed out on anything growing up by himself. Brothers were headaches, and about ninety-four percent of the time, he wanted to bite them.

"I take it back. I don't want to be in your Clan."

"Too late. Leah made us matching T-shirts. Glitter glue was involved. Can't take it back now."

"I hate you."

"Trina lost her whole Clan," Ethan said suddenly.

Inside the bar, she gave her dad a big hug, and they stayed like that for a minute. Something was wrong. She was upset.

Kade sighed. "I know that part."

"Then you know how tough she is. She suffered the pain of all those broken bonds, of everyone she cared about dying, and she's still here. She was watching you the other day, Kade. In that cell? She was sitting there watching you breathe. I never seen a woman more worried about someone. She lost a Clan, and not only did she survive it, but she was brave enough to open herself up to another Clan and un-jaded enough to still care about people."

"Tough girl," Kade murmured, tracking her movement across the bar with a tray of beers for a table of blue-collar boys.

"Yeah. Maybe even tough enough to handle you." Ethan Changed and lifted off the ground with the flap of his wings. A single black feather floated down and landed on the grass beside Kade. He leaned over and picked it up just to make sure it was real...just to make sure he hadn't imagined Ethan.

It wouldn't have been the first time.

You aren't crazy at all.

The biggest tragedy in his life was that Trina was wrong.

SEVEN

"I know you're out there," Trina called. Well, she didn't *know* know. More like, she was hopeful.

She did feel watched, though. The acre of woods around her little one-bedroom cabin was still and quiet. There were no little animal sounds, no breeze rattling dry leaves, no birds settling in for the night.

Sure, it was three in the morning, but still. Usually there was something awake with her when she got home from late nights closing down the bar. She was still getting used to the hours of The GutShot. Her and her dad, Cooper, had only just bought it six months ago. And she was the main one who managed it since her dad was a pilot and ran shipments in and out of these parts as much as he could.

She shifted the bag of frozen burger patties and hamburger buns into her other hand and scanned the woods one more time. "Hello?"

No answer, nothing moved.

It had been three days since she and Kade had been released from the Darby Precinct. Three days since he'd led her up the stairs and to the parking lot where her dad waited on one side and Ethan on the other. Three days since Kade stopped right in the middle of that parking lot, turned on her, gripped her arms, and said, "I can't have fragile things." He'd leaned in like he wanted to kiss her, but paused then released her and walked away without looking back.

That moment haunted her now.

Damn him.

He'd made her pay attention. She'd had her shoulders hunched against the storm of her life, and he'd made her sit up straight and look right at him. He'd made her interested, and it wasn't just being in heat. She didn't only want him in bed. She didn't only want him to take the edge off by fucking for a few minutes. No. She wanted to know everything about him because what he had exposed of himself was raw, gritty, and beautiful.

He was the most interesting man she'd ever met. And the most dangerous because of it.

She missed him—a man she barely knew. She was losing her mind, and she didn't know what to do about it or how to feel less about him.

Disappointed to her bones that he wasn't here, she made her way to the front porch but stood stock-still when she saw what was waiting for her right up against the logs of the house. It was a rocking chair painted in distressed teal. Her cabin was all natural wood, no fancy stains, so the rocking chair was the only pop of color out here.

Teal was her favorite.

Chills consuming her arms, she looked out at the woods. It had to be him, right? Kade did this? Or made this?

She sat down gingerly in it and rocked. It was well-made, didn't creak, was solid as a redwood, and smooth with every movement. She slid her fingertips over a picture carved onto the left arm. It was the outline of a mountain lion, barely visible because it had been painted over.

But when she felt the other arm, there was nothing there, only smooth, painted wood. No way would an artist who made this leave a beautiful piece unbalanced.

She got off the chair and knelt beside it, searching every smooth surface in the porch light. Finding nothing on top, she pushed the chair back and looked underneath. There. On the undercarriage of the seat, there was carved an outline of a wolf howling at the moon.

Holy shit.

Chills rippled up her entire body.

Kade had done this. He'd carved her animal and his onto this chair. And sure, they were separate, but he hadn't been able to help himself. He'd snuck his animal with hers onto the same piece of furniture.

Trina huffed a breath and sat down on the porch.

Separate.

A hollowness filled her. Emptiness. Loneliness. She and Kade were the same...separate from the world around them.

She was destined to eat alone, be alone, and pretend to be tough and happy for the couples around her. No holding hands with someone who wanted to protect her, no rolling over in the middle of the night to find sanctuary from a bad dream in a man's arms.

A tear streaked down her face. This gift was a beautiful heartbreak. She'd been so determined to stay strong, but losing a Clan hurt. It hurt and made her scared, made her think that being alone was the safest way to take care of a heart.

So why did hers still hurt so bad?

She'd watched Ten and Kurt fall in love and become king and queen of the New Darby Clan. She'd watched her dad love her mother deeply when she'd been alive. She'd watched all the shifters in this territory pair up and fix each other, but who was here to fix her? A wolf who wouldn't let himself be close to her.

She deserved better. She deserved nothing at all. She deserved better. She deserved nothing at all.

A sob escaped her and she just…broke down. But pissed at her weakness, Trina blasted her fists against the porch and let a panther scream rip out of her as long and as loud as she could.

And in the distance, very, very far away…a wolf answered her with the most hauntingly beautiful, heart-wrenchingly lonely howl she'd ever heard.

EIGHT

Trina clutched her hot mug of coffee and stared at the rocking chair. It was dawn, and she'd come out here to enjoy the cup on her new chair, just to feel close to Kade, but her seat was already taken by a box wrapped in newspaper.

She inhaled deeply but didn't smell him near.

Bare-footed, Trina padded across the porch to the chair and set the mug on the railing, then opened the present. It was a set of four butter knives. The gently curved blades all matched, but the handles were made from pieces of deer antler. On the end of each was carved an animal. Mountain lion like Trina, Kurt, and her father. A squirrel like Tenlee. A crow like Ethan. And lastly, a wolf. Like Kade.

They'd all been nestled side by side in the box on a piece of velvet, but the mountain lion and wolf were on opposite sides of each other. Separate. Always separate.

She brushed her fingertip against the handle of the wolf knife. They were beautiful. He was giving her little treasures.

The next morning, there was a rough, wooden picture frame with a black and white picture of her behind the bar, leaning over a piece of paper. Had he seen what she'd doodled that day? It had been a wolf. She could almost *almost* make it out in the picture. On the edge of the frame was an outline of a mountain lion's face, but the wolf was harder to find on this one. She had to open up the back. A wolf head had been sketched on the back of the picture.

She clutched it to her chest and scanned the woods, but as always, Kade was a ghost. She was falling in love with a ghost.

On the fourth day, there was nothing.

One the fifth day, there was nothing.

On the sixth day...still nothing.

On the seventh day, there was a little carving of a mountain lion, but no wolf.

Something had happened.

Trina got dressed in her favorite teal tank top, pulled her hair back in a ponytail, put her sunglasses on, and hit the road because Kade wasn't the only one who could stalk. Trina was a good hunter, too.

The roar of her motorcycle echoed through the woods of Corvallis as she wove up the dirt lane toward the address she'd found. Leah owned this place, but as Trina pulled into the clearing, she was stunned by what she saw. It was a mansion, complete with three stories and big white columns around the wraparound porch. The lawn was manicured, and off to the side was Leah in a red polka dot bikini and matching red sunglasses, sipping on a margarita.

Trina settled the motorcycle on its kickstand and waved to Leah, who wore the biggest grin.

"It's ten in the morning, and you already have a margarita," Trina called as she wound through the stone flower boxes of colorful roses.

"It's five o'clock somewhere," Leah sang back.

Trina giggled and took a seat in the bright blue plastic lawn chair beside the tanning werewolf.

"I've been a little stressed," Leah admitted. "And it's my day off from the Hamburger Shack so I figured, while Ethan is working, I would have a party for one out here and watch the humming birds. Look." She pointed to a trio of feeders on the edge of the woods.

There were two tiny birds flittering this way and that as they drank from the different ones.

"Aww," Trina said. "They're so cute, I don't even want to eat them."

Leah frowned at her and shook her head. "Cats," she muttered. "There's canned margs in the cooler."

Why the heck not? Trina didn't have to be into work until six tonight and had no plans.

"Are you here to ask about Kade?" Leah murmured, eyes on the feeders.

"How did you know?" Trina asked.

"He's part of why I'm stressed," Leah said softly.

"What do you mean?"

"He has trouble with Changes. This time he was out in the woods for three days, and he came back sick."

Trina sat up straight in the chair. "Sick how?"

"Head sick. Or maybe heart sick? He looked awful and couldn't stop snarling, and he didn't even make it five minutes into a meal last night before he said he had to Change again. When I went into his room this morning, his bed hadn't been slept in."

"He lives here?"

"Him and me and Ethan. I was going to sell this place because I couldn't afford the property taxes, but now the boys help, and it's a good home for all of us. Or clubhouse, or whatever you call it."

"It's beautiful," Trina said, staring at the house over her shoulder. "Kade isn't here right now?"

"No. Sometimes I make him hang out with me on my days off. He pretends he hates it, but he smiles when he thinks I'm not looking so I'm pretty sure he doesn't really mind. But today he's just disappeared and won't answer his phone or anything. Ethan is really worried. You asked how I knew you were here to ask about Kade."

"Yeah?"

"I want to show you something." Leah stood, toting her margarita. Clad in her little bikini, she sauntered off toward the back of the house.

Trina grabbed her canned margarita, popped the top, and followed directly. In the sprawling back yard, there was a shop. It looked like an old barn but had been kept up well. It was all clean lines and wood stained the same color. It even had flowers in the landscaping out front. But when Trina followed Leah inside, it was anything but tidy. Sawdust covered the floor in piles, tables with different projects littered the space, tools were everywhere. A set of four matching chairs were in different stages. Cans of paint were scattered along the back wall, and there was a bench that covered the length of the left side of the massive shop.

"That's why," Leah murmured, gesturing to the bench.

Trina approached it slowly in awe. There were carvings of mountain lions. And pictures. Photographs. Sketches nailed to the wall in a collage. In the trashcan right beside his work area, Kade had thrown away piles of pictures and carvings and set them on fire. They were charred, but she bent slightly and pulled out one carving from the ashes that was only burned around the edges. It was of a wolf.

Behind her, Leah said, "He doesn't like his animal. He doesn't like what he is."

Trina swallowed hard.

Enough was enough.

She picked up a carving of a mountain lion and

yanked the bottle of wood glue from the counter. And then she glued that wolf and lion together. And while they dried, she wrote on the top page of his sketch book the words *we are not separate,* and placed the carvings on top of it.

"When he comes home, tell him I have a present for him, but he has to come see me to get it."

The smile on Leah's face was slow and steady, and she nodded once. "Are you going to help me fix him?"

Trina shook her head and looked down at the trashcan full of burned wolves. "No. He doesn't need to be fixed. I like him just fine the way he is."

And when she looked back at Leah, the girl's eyes were rimmed with tears and her bottom lip was trembling. But then there was that slow smile again. "You're a good mate."

NINE

Oh, he'd heard Leah going on and on about how he needed to talk to Trina. Her and Ethan both, but they didn't understand. He would kill Trina. Or at the very least, hurt her, and he couldn't do that to her. Admittedly, he was an asshole and selfish by nature, but with her...she felt different to him. Bigger. More important than everyone else. He would rather stick his masturbating hand in a bear trap than see Trina hurt.

The psychopath in him couldn't stop making her presents. It was like a glitch. He'd become addicted to watching her face from the woods when she found his gifts on the rocking chair he'd built for her. Rocking chair. Ha. Did she even realize what he'd really built her? A Christmas tree. A present box. A catch-all for the trinkets he would probably always bring her until his crazy wolf got him killed or locked away.

Trina was sleeping.

He'd been waiting out here for her bedroom light to go off while he fiddled with the carvings she'd glued together. He'd been carrying it in his pocket all day. *We are not separate.* He would keep that note forever just to be reminded of the girl he could've had—if he'd been a normal werewolf.

Why wasn't she scared of him?

That's the part he couldn't figure out. Look at him. He was posted up outside her house every night, waiting for her to drift off to sleep so he could sneak her a present. And when he was Changed, he was running around her woods taking a piss on every tree like he was marking his damned territory. He was clearly hunting her, and she should be scared, so why had she come all the way out to his home, into his shop, and written that letter?

He ran his thumb over the burned wolf. Because *we are not separate.*

He didn't understand her. He didn't understand

himself. He didn't understand anyone.

Tonight's gift, she wouldn't like. He already accepted that. It was just a rock he'd found that had a pretty purple sheen to it, and he'd picked it up for her.

Maybe he would leave it right here so that someday when she was walking through the woods, long after he was locked up or killed, she would find it and have a happy moment.

A twig snapped behind him, and the hairs electrified instantly on the back of his neck. Kade spun with a snarl in his throat, only to find Trina standing there with a big, bright smile on her face. She wore cutoff shorts and a red tank top that made her fair skin look even paler in the moonlight. Over one shoulder, she held one of those cheap bag chairs they sold in every grocery store.

"I got tired of waiting for my present," she chirped as she pulled the chair out of its nylon case. She yanked on the handles until it was chair-shaped and settled it on the dry leaves. And then she squatted by a little blue cooler and pulled out a couple of Bud Lights.

He crouched there wondering how the hell he'd

been snuck up on while she popped the top of the first and held it out for him. "Beer?"

"Uuuuuh…yes?"

"I would've brought you a chair too, but I figured you'd rather stick to your special squatting spot and would decline it anyway."

"My what?"

Trina sat in her chair and pointed to where he was kneeling. "I found that spot yesterday. Seems to be your favorite. It smells like you."

Kade narrowed his eyes and approached, took the beer from her, and took a long swig. Huh. Good little stalker.

She was still holding out her hand, and she wiggled her fingers at him. "Gimme."

"How do you know I have anything for you?" he asked.

"Because that's why you're out here, right? Waiting for me to go to sleep. Well, I don't want to go to sleep. I want to hang out. I've been having bad dreams."

"About what?" he asked.

"I dream that I'm in this car and I'm drowning, but then I wake up."

"Geez, woman. That's horrible."

Trina shrugged. "I've had it since I was a kid. Sometimes I get a break for a few months, but it always comes back and I always wake up gasping for air."

"Do you feel trapped lately?"

In the blue hues of moonlight, Trina's blond brows drew down and made a cute little worry line on her forehead. "Maybe a little."

Kade made his way to the nearest tree and leaned against it. "Why?"

There was a slight smile to Trina's lips when she ducked her gaze. "I don't know."

"Bullshit, you know. You aren't one of those women who doesn't know her own mind."

"Well, I haven't had anyone ask me that before." She fiddled with the unopened tab of her beer. "I guess I'm stressed about the bar. It's still a little new, and me and my dad barely break even on it right now. I'm in a new Clan, and it's an adjustment." She heaved a breath and leveled him with a look. "And I like this man, but he doesn't want to be near me."

Kade took a long sip of the beer, stalling. "This man…you think he likes you back?"

"Yes."

"Why?"

"Because he brings me presents. He thinks about me even when he's not around me. He makes me things. I don't need gifts, and I don't ask for them, but he is thoughtful anyway. He takes care of me in his own way."

"And this man...you aren't scared of what his gifts could mean?"

"No. I'm hopeful of what they mean."

"What do you think they mean?"

"That he likes me the way I like him."

This girl. God, she had his heart beating against his damn sternum. He'd never liked a girl like this. It was terrifying. For him and for her. He should go.

"I didn't bring you a present tonight, Trina. Me being here doesn't mean what you think it does."

And then he turned and walked away.

****

Ghost.

Kade was a ghost when he wanted to be, coming and going as he pleased, haunting her woods—but enough was enough.

"If you walk away right now, don't you even think

of coming back."

Kade halted with his broad back to her. Hot man in jeans that rode low on his hips and a white T-shirt that showed off every curve of his back musculature. Didn't matter how beautiful a body if the mind was poisoned. Didn't matter how attractive a man if he couldn't stick around for something as simple as a conversation.

He turned his head, allowing her to see his profile as he slid a narrow-eyed glance at Trina.

"Just so you know," she murmured, "I don't care about presents. You could never give me another present as long as you know me, and I would still like you."

"If I Changed right now, do you know what would happen?"

"Yes," she answered.

He turned slowly and canted his head to the side. His eyes were almost white and glowing in the moonlight. She should be terrified, but she wasn't.

"What do you *think* would happen?"

"Do you remember our time in the jail?"

Silence stretched between them. On and on until she accepted he wouldn't answer.

"Because I remember," she murmured. "I think about it all the time. Your wolf was mad. He was crazy. Bloodthirsty. He had no emotion but anger, and that was scary, yes, but for me, that's not the part that sticks out the most."

"Which part do you remember the most?"

She put her drink down and stood, then closed the space between them. Breath shaking, she slid her hands up his chest and splayed her fingers, felt the drumming of his heartbeat. And then she whispered, "I think about the man the most. The one who talked to me, felt regret, who clearly accepted his lot in life as a lone wolf. But you're trying, aren't you?" Trina looked up into his eyes and searched his face. "You're trying. You just don't want to admit it. You want more, so you followed your stepbrothers and got protective. You got loyal to your step-mom, and you've stayed close to your dad. You pledged to Ethan's Clan because you want to learn how to stay steady. And you follow me and bring me presents because you want a better life." Trina slid one hand up his stone-hard chest to his neck she touched his whiskers. The growl in his throat wasn't threatening. It was more like the purr in hers. "All of this that you're doing, it isn't just hunting for you. It's signs that you aren't hopeless, and that gives me hope because you're making an effort. And you can't fault a man who keeps making an effort."

"But you can fault a monster when he fails," he rumbled, leaning his cheek into her palm. "And failing means I will hurt you. Do you know what the hardest thing is for a man?"

"Hmm?"

"Hurting the people he loves."

Trina smiled slowly. He hadn't said the words in order—I love you—but he'd just admitted he did. He loved her. She wasn't alone in this. "Your wolf could try to hurt me, sure. It's a risk. But I've decided something."

Kade's eyes drifted to a flyaway lock of her hair, and then he gently pushed it behind her ear. "What did you decide, pretty kitty?"

"If your wolf hurt me...I would hurt him back, make myself safe, because it's what you would want. And then I would forgive him, over and over, because I know the man. You're kind, protective, and thoughtful. The good in you is so much bigger than the bad."

Kade dragged his fingertips up her arm, trailing fire where he touched her skin. "You really believe that?"

Leaning into his touch, she kissed his palm. "Yes," she whispered. "I really do."

Up, up his fingertips went until he gripped the back of her neck. His lips twisted into a feral smile, and her stomach dipped with how sexy he was. Dangerous man who could handle her. She didn't have to be gentle with him. There wasn't anything fragile about Kade.

His lips crashed onto hers, and for a moment, she was shocked with the force of it. With the power that vibrated off his body and blew right through her. He wasn't holding back anymore, and for a second, she was shocked at how much his presence took up every molecule of space. He was Kade. He was the wolf. He was the woods, the stars, the moon, a hurricane. And there was something so addictive about holding the attention of a hurricane. So she threw her arms around his shoulders and held on. The way he kissed her was changing her. She wouldn't be her old self anymore if she gave into her need for him. She would be different from the inside out, and she had no idea what all that entailed. All she knew was that this wasn't some lusty night with a man to relieve the pangs of her heat. It was so much more than lust.

She was burning up under his touch. His hands were rough on her hips, her waist, her neck, her shoulders, then gripping the back of her hair, he began pushing her backward as he kissed her into oblivion.

High.

She was high as a kite on whatever he was doing to her body. He dragged her hips against his, and she could feel it there between them. His erection was so hard and thick. She wanted it—no, needed it.

"Kade, please," she whispered on his lips as he pushed her back against a tree.

"I'll take care of you," he promised.

Every fiber of her body was reaching for him. She couldn't get close enough. She pushed his shirt up over his head, and he helped yank it off the rest of the way. He tossed it into the dirt and pulled off her shirt, then tossed it, too.

His lips were on hers again, moving smoothly like lava over rocks. Tasting her with his tongue. The man could kiss. It was as if he knew exactly what she liked.

He was in complete control, and she was left to enjoy the ride. No thinking, just lost in the moment with him. Kade yanked off her bra and tossed into the woods. As he dropped to his knees, he ripped her jeans down to her ankles, which then joined the clothes mess on the forest floor. He buried his face between her legs, lapping his tongue over and over her clit until she was moaning with every lick and moving with him. His hands gripped her ass so hard with each suck. Fuck, she was already so close.

"Kade, I'm gonna...I'm gonna..."

"Finish," he demanded. And he thrust his tongue deep inside her. Steady. Licking. Hard. All she could do was grip a low-hanging branch above her and hold on as her legs buckled. He held her hips as her body exploded around his tongue. She cried out, and the second his grip softened, she went to her knees, straddling his lap. Kade lifted her and positioned the head of his thick cock right at her entrance, and then he squeezed her hips in a powerful grasp and pulled her down over the length of him until he was buried deep inside her.

She was still having aftershocks when he began moving her up and down his dick. Rough boy. She loved this. He knew just how to handle her. With a snarl in his throat, Kade laid her on her back, never breaking their connection, and then he drew back and rammed into her.

She groaned in ecstasy because it felt so good. He slammed into her again and again. And now another release was building. "Oooooh Kade, it's happening again."

"Good girl," he murmured against her ear, right before he nipped her sensitive lobe and thrust into her again. He was so big, so perfect inside of her. He started to buck into her faster and faster. All she could do was hold tight onto his shoulders when he buried himself deep and froze, his dick pulsing, filling her with warmth. He groaned with every jet he spilled into her, and the throbbing brought on another orgasm. Panting, she clung to him, digging her nails into his back in desperation as she finally, finally found relief with the man who had all of her attention. Who had all of her animal's attention.

As her body pulsed on, Kade laid his teeth on her neck and bit down just enough to cause the perfect amount of pleasure and pain. Then he sucked her neck hard before moving his lips to her ear. "You're mine now, Pretty Kitty."

TEN(TEN)

"What are you so smiley about?" her dad, Cooper, asked.

She hadn't realized he was watching her, so Trina cleared her throat and composed her face. She busied herself with eating a trio of French fries, but yep, that dumb smile was stretching her face again, no matter how hard she tried to keep it off.

"She has a crush on a boy," Leah said unhelpfully as she swished around their table in her fitted pink waitress dress. She set Dad's chicken finger basket in front of him and put her hands on her hips, looking from Trina to Dad to Trina again. "We're basically sisters now," Leah squeaked.

Dad frowned. "I thought that wolf was steering

clear of you."

Stupid smile wouldn't stay off her face! "Well—"

Leah interrupted. "Kade told me this morning he is working on his Changes, and when I asked why, he said, 'None of your damn business,' and when I reminded him we are in the same Clan and he is my maker and everything is my business, he growled a lot and walked outside, but I followed him and promised to make him a macaroni friendship picture of us frolicking through the forest together. When he told me he would quit the Clan if I did, I told him, 'Fine, I won't make you a macaroni picture if you tell me why you are working on your Changes.' Then he said one word." Leah's smile was megawatt as she looked from Trina to Cooper and back again.

Even though Trina had big hopes on what that one word was, it was Dad who took the bait first. "What word?"

"Trina!" Leah said in a high octave that made both Trina and Dad hunch their shoulders and cover their sensitive ears.

Leah clapped her hands over her mouth and then whispered, "Sorry. Still not used to shifter hearing."

Her eyes were glowing silver like Kade's, and

since the lunch rush was hitting the Hamburger Shack, Trina gestured to her face. "Leah, you're gonna have to calm down if you don't want everyone in this town knowing you're a wolf."

Leah glanced around, smile still plastered across her face. "Why would I care about that? I'm a motherfuckin' werewolf. That's so cool!"

Trina snorted and shook her head. "All right, go on with your big bad wolf self."

"Okay, I better get back to work. My best friend Billy is watching me."

"It's Bill!" the cook yelled from the open window to the kitchen.

Trina snorted as Leah sauntered off, humming to herself like she hadn't just been yelled at.

Movement out the front picture window caught her attention. That, or it was her instincts telling her Kade was near because, when she looked up from her half-eaten burger basket, the tall wolf was lowering the tailgate on an old Ford pickup truck. He wore a baseball hat, white T-shirt, and jeans that were threadbare at the knees. Sunglasses covered his eyes, and he hadn't shaved this morning. A toothpick hung from his masculine lips. Lucky, lucky toothpick. He gave a crooked smile to the shop owner, Mr. Owen, who approached him out of the general store. He shook his hand, his triceps rippling. His shirt clung to his shoulders and back as he moved and, holy balls, she knew exactly what he looked like under those clothes. Didn't diminish the celebration that every single hormone in her body was throwing right now. Kade was the hottest guy she'd ever seen. Not that she was staring as he unloaded a trio of rocking chairs out of the bed of his truck. My, what big muscles he had.

Mr. Owen handed him a wad of cash, and Kade pocketed it before he helped the shop owner carry the chairs to the front of his store across the street.

Okay, she had seen all those memes online about the hot handymen, and she wasn't trying to be one of those easily twitter-pated girls, but good God, there was something incredibly sexy about a man who could fix things. And build them. Those chairs were beautiful, polished oak from the look of them. They were different than the chair he'd made for her.

Kade jogged across the street and, holy hell, time slowed. Relaxed fists pumping, smile on his face, white T-shirt suctioned to his Adonis body in the breeze.

"Are you okay?" Leah asked from right beside her.

"Aaah!" she yelped, nearly jumping out of her own skin. "Leah, don't do that!"

"Do what?"

"Sneak up on people!"

"She bumbled over here like a lumbering Rhino," Dad said, staring at Trina like she'd lost her mind, which she had. "Leah almost fell twice and she knocked over a metal napkin holder."

"I like you Cooper," Leah chirped. "You say it how it is."

When Trina turned back to the window, Kade was right there. Right. There. Inches from the glass where she sat with a sinful smirk on his sexy face.

Beside her, Leah was waving like a lunatic. "Hey, Kade! This is so cool. This is that two-way glass, so he can't even see us. He's just able to sense you because you're his mate." She pulled Trina out of her chair and started shoving her toward the door.

"What?" Trina asked.

"What?" Dad called even louder in a booming voice.

"Life-diddlers, eternal partners in crime, modern

day Bonny and Clyde, forever snugglers, the lips made for only Kade's BJs, the one, the only—"

"Leah, what are you doing?" Trina said, trying to struggle out of her iron grip as she shoved her out the front door.

"You are mates, Trina! You've found him! You've found the one! Sure, he is ninety-four percent psychotic, but all that unstable passion was made just for you." Outside, Leah released her and gestured for her to go. "Be free, Trina," she whispered weirdly. "Go find your hopes and dreams."

Trina and Kade stood there staring at her. "Are you having another episode?" he asked Leah.

"Yes," she whispered through the mushiest smile.

Kade sighed. "Sorry about that. She's been on a chick-flick binge for a week. I think she's on her period."

Trina snorted and then laughed, but coughed to cover it up because the smile had fallen from Leah's face.

"My menses is none of your business, Kade. And are you the one who took all my romantic movies from the TV stand?"

"Yep. Those will rot your mind."

"You replaced them with all war movies and old westerns!"

"You're welcome. You can tell Ethan he is welcome, too. Start with Wyatt Earp. It'll change your life."

"Does it have kissing in it?" Leah asked, crossing her arms over her chest. Her cheeks were turning red, and this might have been the first time Trina ever saw the girl frown. "Or I-love-yous, or hand-holding, or a break up and a make up?"

"You don't need all that stuff."

Leah stormed off. "I'm telling Ethan."

"Go on, tattletale! Then he'll know who to thank next time he doesn't have to watch *Never Been Kissed* for the millionth time in a row."

"You're the worst Clan-mate!"

Kade's expression was absolutely unremorseful as he watched Leah walk away.

"She's going to kick you out of the Clan," Trina murmured, turning to face him.

"Good. I'm better off a Lone Wolf anyway." But his voice lacked conviction, and he was still wearing that crooked smile that said he was more teasing than serious. "Hey," he rumbled, slipping his hands to her waist and bringing her in close.

The butterflies in her stomach were on a rampage as he leaned in. The bill of his hat was in the way so she pushed it off him and slipped her hands around his shoulders. Was he really going to kiss her right here in front of everyone? This was right in the middle of town, at midday, and the hub of gossip.

But nope...nope, he didn't care. Because his smile pressed right onto hers, and his lips softened as he angled his head to the side. His mouth moved against hers so easily, like they'd been born to be connected just like this. When his tongue slipped past her lips, her body reacted. Nipping his bottom lip, she pressed harder against him. He wrapped his arms around her waist, hugged her so tight it was hard to inhale.

But who cared about breathing right now? Kade was kissing her. He was giving her this normal couple moment just like everyone else got, just like she'd always wanted.

And then she heard it—the growl rattling his throat. It got louder and louder until he eased back and rested his forehead against hers. He was gritting his teeth so hard his jaw was clenched.

"Hey," she whispered, pulling back. She took the

sunglasses off his face to reveal his tightly closed eyes. "Look at me."

He eased them open, and they were blazing such a light silver there was almost no color other than his pupil.

"You look really pretty today," he said in a voice that sounded a bit like a demon's.

Butterflies, bats, and birds were a hurricane inside of her.

"I've been checking you out, too," she admitted, dragging her hands down his chest.

"It's a good surprise seeing you here."

"I'm eating lunch with my dad."

Kade straightened his spine and searched her face. "Your dad is here?"

"Yep. He's inside."

The growl died in his throat. Kade pulled his baseball hat from her hand, then put it on her head, the bill backward. "You're so fuckin' cute. I'm gonna go meet your dad." Before she could respond, Kade pulled her by the hand toward the door.

"Okay, this is hot."

"What is?" he asked through a frown as he held the door open for her.

"You wanting to meet my dad. And not being intimidated by it."

"Why wouldn't I want to meet him? He's one of your people."

Okay. Simple as that then. Dad was important to her so Kade was making him important to him, too. The second he walked inside, Kade strode right over to Dad and offered his hand for a shake.

And as she watched Kade swallow his unsteady growl to greet her dad, shake his hand like a man, look him in the eyes, and show him respect...she had this moment.

Dad was smiling at something Kade said, nodding his head, and Kade looked back at her with an expression that asked, "Why aren't you here beside me?" Dad looked impressed and shocked all at once, and the two most important men in her life were looking at her with matching smiles. She wanted to cry, in a good way. She'd never dated anyone who wanted to meet her dad, even if she'd begged them. And Kade had wanted this. She hadn't even had to ask. He just...met her needs.

And right now, in this moment, she realized she loved him, and the love she felt was irreversible. It wasn't caused by her heat, wasn't caused by lust, wasn't just a crush on a boy. Her heart just decided he was it, and she knew down to the marrow in her bones she would never want another like she wanted Kade. Wanted his safety, wanted his happiness, wanted his steadiness, wanted his body, wanted his soul—all the good and bad parts of it. And most of all, she wanted him to feel irreversible love for her, too.

They waved her over, and in a daze she sat by Kade and listened to him talk easily to her dad. He was growling still, but Dad wasn't making him pay for that instability. He wasn't calling him out. He just kept talking like the threatening noise wasn't there.

Kade ordered his own hamburger and snuck Leah money for the whole bill before she or Dad could pay. As they sat there chatting, Kade slid his hand over her thigh, and she wrapped her arms around his bicep happily.

I've waited my whole life for him.

Kade stopped what he was saying mid-sentence and jerked his attention to her. "What did you say?"

"Hmm?" She kissed his shoulder and said, "I didn't say anything."

His teeth showed in a flash of a smile, and then he

leaned in and murmured against her ear, "I've been waiting for you, too."

ELEVEN

The sound of the saw drowned out Kade's snarling. That's why he had been drawn to tools in the first place. Loud noises made him feel almost normal. He could work alone and pretend his wolf wasn't a raving lunatic, growling at a saw just because it existed. He didn't wear earplugs when he worked. He wanted to hear the sound of metal sawing through wood. It was his only therapy. It used to be the only part of his life he had any control over because, when he was in the shop, restoring something or building it from nothing, he felt the most at peace a monster could feel.

Or that's the way it used to be before Trina. Now she was his therapy. She had been for weeks. She was his motivation, his peace. But working wood helped in the hours between seeing her. And this work was an income. There was now a drive inside him to take care of Trina. Oh, that lion never asked since she was independent as fuck, but if she ever slipped, he wanted to be there to prop her up. And that meant saving. It meant putting money away for help if the bar ever went into a dip, money for presents…money for a ring someday because, hell yeah, he was reaching for the damn stars at this point. He would one-hundred percent go crazy or die before he went shopping for diamonds, but it was still fun to think about, still a goal he wished he could achieve, still a gift he would give his bones to be able to give her someday. Trina deserved everything.

He had three orders for matching chair sets sitting in his email right now but was falling behind thanks to the damn wolf. He took the body for too long. Every time Kade woke up, he'd lost days. He'd lost time. He'd lost life. Too much of his time was spent as a wolf. Which sucked for lots of reasons, but most of all he missed Trina. And he missed his shop.

He loved the way it smelled in here. Like sawdust and oil and metal and smoke, paint and wood stain…

And one familiar wolf.

Kade turned on his stool. Behind him, Mick, the Second in the Wulfe Clan, was standing in the doorway, blond hair mussed, a motorcycle helmet dangling from his hand, and a dead-eyed stare directed right at Kade. Kade flipped the switch on the saw mid-cut and sniffed the air. There was something else on the breeze, just below the scent of dominant werewolf. It was sickness. Mick was sick. His wolf was unsteady, and the man's eyes were changing from brown to green and back again. Kade knew all about crazy wolves.

"You're pretty fuckin' brave to stare down a beast with a taste for blood as big as mine. Dumb as a post to come into my territory, too." He pulled off his gloves and tossed his baseball hat onto an old wooden chair in the corner. Shaking his hair out, he asked, "What the fuck do you want, Mick? Besides a slow death?"

"You've been causing us problems. Problems. You've been causing *me* problems." Mick had a tick. He twitched his head twice hard and growled something indecipherable to himself.

"Maybe I'm not the problem," Kade said.

"We're considering peace with every Clan in the territory, but we just can't seem to get you to shut the fuck up or stop fighting."

Kade smiled, canted his head, and then softly he howled, "Owooooo."

"I'm here to give you a choice. Option one, you come into the Clan. You've messed with the entire pecking order every fight. We need it steadied out, and something tells me you won't quit fighting just because we ask politely."

"Ha! Are you fuckin' serious? You want me to join your Clan? I would rather piss on an electric fence. Listen carefully, Mick, because I won't repeat myself. I'll die before I ever pledge to a werewolf Clan."

Mick twitched his head twice again. The hand that held the motorcycle helmet shook. "Well, that brings me to option two."

Kade huffed a laugh. He was already so fuckin' ready to fight just seeing this asshole in his shop. Inside, his wolf was snarling to be released, and his arms and legs were already tingling with the first signs of the Change. There would be no stopping it now but...*go on Mick. Give the wolf even more reason to kill you for trespassing on his territory*. "And what's option two?" He already knew the answer. He just needed Mick the Prick to say it out loud to get his wolf bloodthirsty.

"Option two, you die. Either way, you won't be messing with the hierarchy of my Clan anymore."

"You and what army are gonna kill me, Mick? You couldn't do the job with your entire Clan at the GutShot. I damn near killed your Alpha, so tell me," he barked out, "why the fuck are you really here?"

Mick lifted his chin higher and stared down his nose at Kade with an empty smile. "I was ordered to give you options. You picked option two, just like I knew you would."

Mick's eyes blazed bright green as he pulled a Glock from the back of his jeans.

Coward. Mick was a fuckin' coward. He had a wolf inside of him, and he brought a gun? Weak. Kade was going to kill him.

Time slowed to a crawl as Mick lifted the weapon. His finger was already on the trigger. His feral eyes were dancing as though he couldn't wait to pull it. As though he couldn't wait for revenge for all those times Kade had bested him and his Clan.

They should've been stronger.

Kade let the wolf have his body and, shhhhhit, it hurt. When the wolf came out enraged, it was like falling into a fire. He was fire. He was fire and death and everything dark. Kade used to hate it, but in this moment, he embraced the darkness. It was time to use the poison inside of him as a weapon.

He hit the sawdust-covered ground on all fours and dug his claws in, bolting straight for that asshole. There was this satisfying look of shock on Mick's face. He hadn't expected Kade to charge him. That much was clear from the way his eyes went round.

Better aim good, Mick. One bullet ain't gonna save you from me.

With a ripping snarl, Kade bunched his muscles and sailed through the air right for Mick.

And Mick...that coward...that weak wolf...

He pulled the trigger.

TWELVE

Biting her thumbnail, Trina frowned at the door to the bar. Her shift had ended an hour ago. Kade had planned to pick her up and take the motorcycles on a trip to Corvallis, maybe eat lunch along the way. She'd been so excited when he'd asked her, but he hadn't shown up. It wasn't like him. Sure, she had to get used to days at a time when he was out in the forest running around as a wolf and unable to Change back, but he usually told her before he was going to go off the rails. Or she could tell from the shaky control he had over the wolf. When it got worse, he was usually close to a Change. But when she'd left his bed this morning, he'd been calm and relaxed. His eyes had even been their human color when he'd walked her to her motorcycle and kissed her goodbye.

Trina had been harboring this awful feeling in her gut all morning—like something was wrong. It was that animal instinct that roughed her fur up the wrong way. Like that clammy feeling right before a big storm that told her to take shelter.

But she'd pushed those feelings to the side while she worked because everything was fine. Kade was doing better with Changes, and Dad was doing good, on a flight to pick up supplies for the Two Claws Ranch. Ten and Kurt were happy as little clams when they'd come in for lunch earlier with Kurt's little boy, and the bar had actually turned a little profit this month. Life was good. She needed to stop waiting for that other shoe to drop and just accept that she was all right. That she was allowed to be happy without any strings attached.

It was probably just the loss she still felt. When the Darby Clan had made their decision and got themselves killed, she'd had to accept that the ache in her chest was a part of her now. That emptiness was something to get used to. But today, it felt bigger, and she didn't want to go back to feeling scared of letting people in. She didn't want to go back to being terrified of loss. Trina wanted to keep moving forward.

He was just running late.

Probably just lost track of time while he was working. He was like that. Very driven. That woodshop out behind the Blackwood Clan house was like Kade's church. That's where he found sanctuary, so she should just call him again and see if he picked up.

She hit his number and waited as it rang and rang.

Well…okay…maybe he had his phone turned down and the music up. She imagined his phone on his workbench in between piles of tools, the screen lighting up as she called but the vibration of the call lost in the noise of a rock song. And then she imagined Kade in there working away without a shirt on, sweat dripping slowly down his perfect chest and abs. And then her daydream turned to him pouring a bottled water over his head in slow motion with the saturated sunlight behind him and, holy shit, she needed him to give her some relief.

I need dat dick, she texted, smiling at her own wit

as she hit *send*. Just to let him know she meant business, she glanced around quick, checking to make sure no one was paying a lick of attention to her. She drew her arms in and squished her cleavage together in her V-neck shirt and then took a selfie real fast and sent that to him as well. She wasn't a man-chaser anymore. She, Trina Luna Chapman, was now a bona fide man-catcher.

And when her phone dinged with the answering text, she grinned a feline smile as she lifted it to her face. Boobs always did the trick with that wily wolf.

She was so prepared for some witty, dirty banter from Kade, she didn't understand the words of the text on her glowing cell phone screen. It wasn't from Kade. It was from Leah.

Gun.

Kade's gone.

Blood everywhere.

Dead wolf.

"W-what?" she murmured aloud. Heart beating against her ribs, she connected a call to Leah.

She picked up on the first ring, but Trina could barely hear her between the sobbing.

"Just came home—sob—everything smells like

pennies—the grass is wet—blood on the sawdust—Trina!— there's blood on the sawdust! And a big wolf. He's been mauled. He's just staring back at me—sob—there's something in the woods—sob—I can feel something awful out there—sob—it's talking to my wolf—sob—I don't know what to do!"

Trina was already running for the door. "Leah, Leah, stop! Breathe, girl. The dead wolf. Tell me it's not Kade," she demanded as her shoes hit the parking lot pavement at a sprint.

"I don't know."

"Leah!"

"I don't know! It's gray and cream like Kade's but the blood smells different. It's totally torn up. It's hard to tell anything." A long snarl ripped through the phone. "Trina—Trina—*snarl*—I think I'm going to be sick."

"No, you aren't. You're about to Change. Where's Ethan?"

"On a job out in Stevensville. He isn't picking up or answering my texts. Where are you?" Another growl rattled through the phone and then a groan of pain. "Trina. Trina? Are you close? I don't feel good."

"Don't Change! Leah, listen to me!" Trina threw

her leg over the seat of her bike and revved the engine. "I'm headed to you. Don't you disappear into those woods. We don't know what's out there! You can't Change alone right now."

There was a grunt of pain, and then the phone clicked and went dead.

"Leah? Leah? Fuck!" she yelled, yanking on her helmet.

Trina blasted out of the parking lot like a rocket. Her bike was deafening against her sensitive eardrums as she zoomed onto the main road. She only had a month of riding under her belt, but fuck it. If Trina crashed, she was a shifter. She would survive...probably.

Please don't be Kade, please don't be Kade, please don't be Kade!

There was an old work truck in front of her, going way too slow. The wind whipped against her face as she hit the throttle and pulled to the center stripe. A semi was coming from the other way, no room to pass. Shit. She eased off and rode the tailgate for a few seconds before she muttered, "Fuck it," and hit the throttle again. She whipped her sportster onto the rumble strips and then passed the truck on the shoulder. He was cussing out the window when she rode by, but she didn't care. Leah was out in those woods with something bad, and Kade...Kade... Tears of frustration burned her eyes, but Trina had no time for weakness right now. She was a cat of action.

It was all she could do not to reach for her phone and bring in every allied shifter in the known territory down on Leah's land and snuff out whatever had hunted Kade... Kade...Kade...oh, God. With every fiber of her being, Trina knew she wouldn't be okay if the dead wolf was him. That's what this awful empty feeling was in the pit of her stomach, right?

Was it another broken bond? Oh, God, Oh, God...

She took the turn onto Leah's dirt road driveway and spewed dust as she steadied out. The fine hairs on her arms stood straight up as she felt the darkness in the woods that Leah had described. A snarl rippled through her body. The cougar wanted out. The animal inside of her wanted to defend herself. She wanted to survive whatever was happening here.

There was evil in these woods.

Heart in her throat, she slammed on the brakes and skidded to a stop in front of Leah and Ethan's mansion. It was cloudy today, and the place looked haunted, empty. Trina cut the engine and froze, listening for any movement, any heartbeats. There was one, hammering as hard as hers, racing hers.

Trina dismounted and sniffed the air. Pennies, just like Leah said. Blood. Lots of it.

Under the porch, Leah whined. Big ol' werewolf hiding under a house? Yeah, whatever was in the woods was bad.

Trina set her helmet on the seat of her Harley and fought back the urge to Change. The monster in the woods was calling to her like a damn siren.

"Come on," she murmured as she passed the place Leah had dug out under the porch. A massive black werewolf with silver eyes slunk out from under the house and scanned the woods before she loped beside Trina, her ears and tail down, her attention on the woods.

For comfort, Trina rested her hand on the back of the wolf.

Trina would've left Leah under that house if it had made her feel safe, but right now she was selfish. She couldn't look at the dead wolf alone. If it was Kade, she was about to break, so she would put that burden on Leah and ask for forgiveness later.

The scent of blood thickened the air and made it hard to breathe. The wolf had fallen right at the entrance to the woodshop. She could see the mangled body from a distance but couldn't tell...couldn't tell...

Trina jogged, then ran. She skidded to a stop right beside the enormous wolf and dropped to her knees as she searched the body. Gray fur, cream tips, just like Kade...but this wasn't Kade. Gold-green eyes stared back at her. The eyes of Mick, Second of the Wulfe Clan.

"It's not him," she chanted in a thick whisper. "It's not him."

Tears streaked down her cheeks, and she reached out to Leah for comfort but Leah wasn't close. She was pacing back and forth, her tail tucked. Back and forth, back and forth, putting herself between Trina and the haunted woods.

There was a Glock beside her. She leaned closer and sniffed. Discharged. And the blood splatters leading out from the shop weren't Mick's.

Stupid fucking wolf. He'd come here to murder Kade, but he'd failed.

That meant the monster in the woods was Kade.

He was hurt. And an injured predator with

nothing to lose was the most dangerous of all.

The Wulfe Clan had done this. They'd snapped the man she loved. They'd hurt him.

Rage shaking her hands, Trina pulled her cell from her back pocket and called Darius.

"What?" he answered.

"Mick failed."

There was silence on the other end so she said, "Did you hear me, you cowardly fuck? I said Mick failed. Your Second is dead, and now you've got one helluva monster to deal with. And I'm not talking about Kade. I'm talking about me. I know what you did. Kade fucked with your Clan's rankings, didn't he? He beat you, and you're nursing your injuries and your pride, so you sent an assassin. You won't be able to find a hole deep enough to hide from me, so we can do this one of two ways. You can grow some fucking balls and meet us face to face, or we can hunt you down and kill you sniveling wolves while you run away with your fucking tails tucked."

"Careful, kitty. I think you've forgotten who you're talking to—"

"No, Darius, I know exactly who the fuck I'm talking to! Coward. Murderer. You've been a growing thorn in this town for years. I've watched. I've waited. I've sat back observing you, because that's what cougars do. We hunt patiently. And you just kept fucking up. And then you got it in your head you were going to murder my mate on our own territory? You've lost your fuckin' mind."

"Time and place, bitch."

"No bitches here, Darius. I'm a lion. I think it's you who forgets who the fuck you're talking to. Three nights from now works for me, the edge of Blackwood Crow territory."

Darius huffed a breath. "Little girl, you have no idea what you've just done."

"Oh, I know what I've done. You used me as bait to draw Kade to my bar to fight him. And when that didn't work, you sent your Second with a gun to kill him. Chicken-shit wolves. I know exactly what I'm doing. Kade will be the bullet, and I'll be the trigger. I've declared war, asshole. Go get laid, eat a good steak, and enjoy your last couple of nights breathing."

Trina hung up the phone and looked up to find Leah staring back at her, silver eyes churning, her hair raised up like a mohawk down her back. A long, hollow-sounding howl lifted on the breeze, and chills rippled up Trina's arms as Leah let off a long snarl.

Monster.

Monster.

Monster.

The Wulfe Clan had turned her mate into a monster. They'd crossed a line they couldn't uncross, and the cost to them would be Trina's infinite fury.

She made another call.

Her mountain lion Alpha, Kurt, answered. "Hey."

"I've got a dead wolf on Blackwood Crow property."

There was a second of silence and then, "Do you need a cleaner for the body? And whose fault is it?"

"It's on the Wulfe Clan. Mick's dead, but he shot Kade on his way to Hell. I don't know how bad it is, but I can feel Kade, and something is wrong. Really, really wrong. He's close. Probably watching me and Leah from the woods."

"What do you need?"

"Alliances."

"You're calling a war?"

"Yes."

"Does Kade feel like your mate?"

"Yes." She choked on the word and blinked back

burning tears, then tried again in a stronger voice. "Yes, he's mine."

"Then he has the fealty of our Clan. Two Claws Clan, too. I'll talk to Hairpin Trigger and the Warmaker. The Blackwoods and Red Dead Mayhem are up to you. Don't go in those woods alone, Trina. I'll be there as soon as I can. I'll make calls. We'll all be there soon."

The call disconnected, and Trina let the phone drop into her lap. There was too much blood from Kade. She couldn't wait for help to arrive. She needed to see with her own eyes that he was okay. The scent of his blood was as thick as the dead wolf beside her. Strong mate, but he wasn't invincible.

Trina stood and peeled her shirt over her head as she made her way straight for the part of the woods that emanated the most darkness.

"Go back under the house, Leah," Trina told her. "Everything is going to be okay."

Leah whined and slunk in front of her, almost tripping Trina. With a sigh, she knelt down and cupped the wolf's face. "He's mine. He's hurt. I'm the only one who has a shot at reaching him. When help gets here, tell them what happened. If I'm not back before dark, send in the crows."

The black wolf laid there watching her as Trina stood, stepped over her, and stripped out of her clothes. And when she reached the edge of the woods, she heaved a sigh and hesitated. It felt like polar opposite magnets. Like the woods were trying to keep her out. Another howl ripped through the air. But the wolf was calling her in. Push, pull, push, pull.

Trina filled her lungs with air and let the mountain lion inside of her shred her body. Three seconds of pain, and then she had weapons. Teeth, claws, agility, power.

Don't go in those woods alone. Kurt had made the mistake of not making that an Alpha order.

Trina placed one paw in front of the other and stalked into the forest.

Kade was hers. Monster or not, she couldn't leave him out in those woods alone.

THIRTEEN

Pain.

Rage.

Pain.

Rage.

Confusion.

It was hard to focus. The more Kade moved, the more it hurt, but then the fury would hit again, and he couldn't sit still. He'd been calling for a pack he didn't rule. He'd been calling for a Clan who wouldn't answer. The she-wolf he'd made, Leah, had hidden under the house. And then the blond girl had shown up and confused him even more. She was familiar. She was his. No…no. Nothing was his. He was rogue. He was alone. He was a lone wolf. His only job was to exist and to kill.

But he'd watched that girl drop to her knees beside his kill. She'd cried. He could see the tears dripping from her fragile human jaw as she'd mourned that asshole who hurt Kade. She wasn't his. The pain in his shoulder was nothing compared to the ache in his chest as he watched that girl cry over his prey. But why? Why did he care? She was a girl, and he was a beast, and they didn't fit. Clearly. Her feelings were fragile. She went soft for the things that hurt Kade, and it only made him more confused and angrier.

Something bad was happening to his body. He let off another howl. He needed support, or to kill something, or to have a Clan kill alongside him, or to die. He didn't know which.

A leaf moved beside him and, on reflex, he snapped at it. The pain that burned through his shoulder at the motion made him flinch hard, and that movement hurt, too. Fuck, this wasn't good. He wanted to kill anything that moved. He wanted to shred everything. The snarling in his throat became constant. He tried to find a more comfortable position, but the fire in his body only grew hotter. He couldn't see straight. The edges of his vision were starting to get blurry, and the trees were starting to blend together.

Right through the shoulder.

Couldn't put weight on that paw at all.

Choking on the scent of his own blood.

The mossy rock under him was cool, but it didn't give him the relief he'd hoped for, so he stood again and limped mindlessly down the incline, across boulders and felled logs covered with moss. He loved these woods. They were familiar and comfortable, and now they would be where he died. Alone.

He tossed his head back once more and let a howl shred through him.

But this time, he was answered.

A panther scream echoed through the woods. She was close. Good. Fighting would take his mind off dying.

He limped faster, spurred on by the bloodlust. The only thing that could help him now was making something else hurt as much as he hurt.

Through the trees, a mountain lion sauntered gracefully toward him. For a moment, he paused. There was a little voice inside his head, annoying as a gnat, saying, *"Don't fight her. She's special."*

That was the weak side of him. Sometimes he liked to talk, but all that voice ever had to say was "Stop," or "Don't do that," and he was a motherfucking wolf. He was top of the food chain and could do whatever he pleased, no boring human logic required. That voice could piss off.

A lion fight was exactly what would feed the rage pulsing inside him.

He gave her a smile. And by smile, he drew his lips back over his teeth so she could see her death coming.

The cat was stunning, sleek with muscles and striations sitting right under her skin as she moved toward him. The woods came alive with the pitter-patter of a rain shower. Gloomy day to die, cat.

But she kept coming straight for him. Whiskers twitching, massive paws flattening against the moss with every step, ears erect like she wasn't afraid at all. Her golden eyes were steady on him, her pupils little pinpoints, her tan coat becoming spotted with rain drops. She had black around her mouth, contrasting with her white chin, and when she drew her lips back from her canines, he had to appreciate them. They were like long, curved daggers.

She was a beautiful weapon, and if she bested him, it would be an honorable death. Much better than the bullet of a coward's gun.

Kade charged.

****

Kade was a mangled mess. His shoulder was matted with red, and he wasn't putting weight on one leg. She was shocked he was still standing at all. It was a testament to how strong he really was. There was this moment when she thought he recognized her. He was descending a mossy rockface and paused to look her right in the eyes. And for a split second, the hate disappeared. There was only pain. Only vulnerability. But then his face twisted with rage, his ears flattened, his muzzle wrinkled with a menacing growl, and he ran right for her on all four legs, as if he wasn't hurt at all. And holy hell, even injured, Kade was as quick as a cobra strike.

Kade was massive, bigger than any other wolf she'd ever seen, and he was closing in on her with the promise of death churning in his silver eyes.

Oh no. Oh no, oh no.

With a hiss, Trina launched herself up a tree. Not

fast enough, though. Teeth latched onto her tail, and she was yanked back to the ground with such force the air was knocked out of her. Gasping in shock, she boxed him across the face with her claws extended, and he staggered to the side.

The wolf swayed and tried to steady itself, but his front leg gave, and he stumbled.

She knew predators. Give him her back, and his adrenaline would dump into his system for round two. He wouldn't be able to help himself. Even hurt, he would have to chase her. So she backed up, belly on the moss until her throbbing tail touched the tree she'd tried to escape up. And then she prepared for a brawl. There was nothing to do but stand her ground.

The growl rattling her throat felt like it went on for hours, but maybe it was only minutes, or seconds even. His chest was heaving, and he swayed again and went down hard. He didn't whine, didn't wince in pain, just laid there. Kade without any fight in him meant something terrible. He'd run out of energy too fast. Lost too much blood.

This was her chance to get up the tree and out of range of those teeth. Her tail hurt so bad, and she knew what he was capable of if he got a second wind.

She looked up at the towering spruce and considered it.

But Kade's breathing was too shallow, and she couldn't leave him if she tried.

Just like when she braved the woods, she put one paw in front of the other, knowing how bad this could hurt.

FOURTEEN

This was it.

This was the end of his life.

Kade had always known it would come too early. He'd know it since he was a pup.

Kade had never in a million years thought he would go at the teeth of a she-lion, though. The big cat stalked closer and closer, her head lowered. That animal was a brick house. She'd knocked him off his hunt with one slap of her paw.

Normal wolves would feel fear at the end, but he'd never been a normal wolf. Fear wasn't an emotion he possessed. Resilience, fight, and don't-quit grit was all he knew.

And as the cougar approached, he huffed a

wolfish laugh in the face of his own death.

She paused just out of teeth range. *Come on, kitty. Don't get scared on me now. Finish it.*

But she didn't. She did something he would never understand.

She touched him. Gently. There was no pain as she pressed her nose against his neck. He waited and waited for a bite on his jugular that didn't come. What was she waiting for, this beautiful angel of death? But when she opened her mouth, it wasn't those long, dagger teeth that touched his neck. It was her tongue. He winced as she licked down to his shoulder.

She was...she was...cleaning him.

The devil in him thought for a second that this was his chance, gather enough strength and bite her. But there was that voice again. Weak and soft, but the wolf could hear it just fine in the quiet of the woods. *Don't fight her. She's special.*

The snarl died in his throat as muscle by muscle, he relaxed under the soothing touch of the lion. She was...special. Yes. It took someone special to touch him. He'd never been touched kindly in all his existence. This body had been built to kill. The only touch he'd known had caused pain, but not here. Not now. Not in the shadows of the towering pines.

He tried to lift his head, but his whole body was cold like ice and didn't work right.

At least he wasn't alone at the end. She was giving him a gift that was bigger than he deserved.

The mountain lion curled her body around his. She was so warm. So soft. Such a contrast against his cold body and course fur. Beauty and the beast. The first caring touch, and it came in the last minutes of his life. Fuckin' typical.

It was getting hard to keep his eyes open.

There was a popping sound, and then his body was jostled and pulled off the ground. With a sigh of agony, he lifted his head just enough to look into the face of the girl. No longer a lion, she was the one with the bright green eyes who had cried over the body of that dead wolf. And now she was crying over Kade. Her tears joined the raindrops in his fur. Her blond hair was plastered to her cheeks from the rain. Brave girl, holding him so close to her naked body like this. Strong girl for being able to lift him at all.

She picked her way down the slick rocks, and he wished he could stay longer. He wished he could be with her until she got out of these woods. He wished he could see her safe home, but being a protector had never been his fate.

Fuck. He wished he had more time. The girl was interesting. The animal in her had cleaned him. Warmed him. He wished he could have more of that.

Because the girl wasn't an angel of death after all.

She wasn't an angel at all, because angels didn't cry over monsters like him.

"Don't leave," she pleaded in a ragged whisper as she buried her face against his fur and gripped him even tighter to her chest. "Please, Kade. I'll never be okay if you leave."

Love—that's what her words meant, right? The weak human part of him had gotten her to love him.

Lucky sonofabitch.

He kept his eyes open as long as he could just to see her face as she carried him through the woods. Tears and determination. Eyes glowing the color of the moss. So beautiful.

Please let me live, he begged whatever powers were listening. *Let me live and I'll be different. I'll be a protector. I'll be her protector.*

To the sound of her sobbing, right before the

world went dark, Kade looked up at the sky and saw the crows.

FIFTEEN

Trina was numb by the time she made it back to the edge of the clearing. She should've been shocked by all the motorcycles and cars skidding to a stop in the front yard, but she was exhausted, heartbroken, and the majority of her focus was on the beating of her mate's heart.

That sound was more important than anything in the world.

She stumbled in the mud on fatigued legs. Kade was massive. She had her shifter strength, but he was dead weight. Dead. Weight. She couldn't tell if her cheeks were damp from tears or rain.

There were people running for her. Rike? Ethan? Hairpin Trigger? Kurt, Leah, Bailey... Red Dead

Mayhem was pulling up on Harleys. Ramsey. The Warmaker…

She nearly went down again. Her feet were all cut up from the rocks. They should hurt, but all she felt was a dull throbbing with each step.

She could only imagine what these people saw. They looked so worried as they ran for her.

Mascara running down her cheeks, hair stuck to the sides of her face, pale as a sheet. Who cared? Not her. She was losing Kade.

Losing him.

Nothing was fair, and nothing would be okay.

Bum-bum bum-bum.

A sob escaped her as Ethan reached her first.

"Let me help," he murmured, taking Kade's body from her.

"No," she said. "No, no, I don't want anyone to touch him." She didn't know what she was saying. "He's—he's—he's—"

"He's yours, Trina. I'm gonna go fix him, okay? You did good, but we have to fix him now."

Trina nodded as everyone left her but Leah. The girl came and stood next to her in the rain and squeezed her hand. "Trina?" she whispered.

Hairpin Trigger was running beside Ethan, holding a rag on Kade's neck and Ethan was barking out orders she didn't understand. Everyone was yelling. The words didn't make sense except for two.

"Breathe, Kade!" Ethan yelled out, desperation tainting his voice.

And those two, pleading words, begging his stepbrother to live, broke something inside of her. Trina's face crumpled.

When her shoulders sagged, Leah asked again, "Trina?"

"Yeah?" she croaked out.

Leah hugged her from the side and rested her face on her shoulder. "You did so good. You brought him back. He's the strongest wolf in the whole world, raised by Ethan and Rike's mom, so he's practically a Blackwood Wolf. He's going to be okay."

"Leah?"

Leah laid a little kiss on her shoulder and snuggled her cheek against her skin. "Yes, best friend?"

"Your boobs are on my arm."

"Nudity is natural," Leah whispered, still nuzzling her. "We're shifters. It's the best part of all this."

Trina wiped her eyes and sighed. "You're really weird."

"Thank you," Leah said in a mushy voice.

"Come on, weirdo. I want to be in that room."

"You do?"

Trina nodded as she un-suctioned herself from Leah's rain-soaked embrace. "This isn't the first time."

"You've been in rooms with injured shifters before?"

"Lots and lots," she said sadly. "My first Clan made a lot of bad decisions, and they died for them. They declared wars in waves. Sometimes when they came home hurt, I'd hold vigil, hoping they pulled through. The Clan didn't learn their lesson. They kept picking and picking, just like the Wulfe Clan does. And then me and my dad sat in the room trying to save Kurt when he was sick."

"You mean succeeding."

"Hmm?" she asked numbly as she padded through the muddy yard behind the crowd filing into Leah and Ethan's house.

"You didn't just *try*, Trina. You *succeeded* in saving Kurt." Beside her, Leah's eyes blazed the same silver as Kade's when he got real determined about something. "You got good magic, Trina. Go save Kade, too."

Trina tried to smile at her, but she didn't really have control of her emotions right now. It might have been a grimace for all she knew. In a daze, she walked up the porch stairs where the crowd of big shifters parted for her. Hands touched her back, her hair, her hands, her shoulders. They were comforting her in their own way, in the way their animals demanded. The edges of her vision were dark and blurry, and her focus was on putting one foot in front of the other, pushing herself closer to her mate. If he stopped fighting, today would be the worst day of her life.

She walked through the kitchen to the hallway that led to the east wing where Kade had claimed a room. A few shifters posted up beside the door, nodded to her and made room for her to pass. The handle was cold under her palm as she turned it and opened the door.

Inside was a scene she would never forget as long as she lived. Kade's wolf was lying on the bed. The pillows had been thrown to the ground, and Ethan and Hairpin Trigger blocked most of his body as they worked. On the bed, Rike and Kurt were holding down the wolf. When Ethan wiped his hair out of his way, there was blood on his hands. Kade's blood. A low snarl rattled her throat before she could stop it.

"Trina, we won't be able to work with you at our backs if you can't control the lion," Ethan said without turning around.

"I'm fine."

Ethan cast a quick, fiery look at her over his shoulder before tossing a piece of mangled, bloody metal to the ground. *Tink, tink, tink.* The bullet landed inches from her toes, and slowly, she knelt and picked it up. It had left a red scuff on the wood floor.

"Come on, man," Rike muttered, his body jerking with whatever he was doing to Kade. "Show a damn sign of life. Mom's gonna kill us if you die."

Trina didn't want to know what they were doing. Not even a little part of her wanted to peek over their shoulders. From the bottom drawer, she pulled out a pair of black cutoff shorts and grabbed one of Kade's Harley T-shirts from the top one. She pulled it on and sniffed the collar. Smelled like him—the human half, who was stuck and hurting in the wolf's body right now. She put the bullet in her pocket because that would be her fuel when she faced the Wulfe Clan.

Kade was going to be avenged.

Following an explosive yelp, Kade turned into a hurricane on the bed, thrashing, eyes white and empty. The boys were yelling, especially Ethan, who kept ordering him to stay still. It was an Alpha command, but Kade wasn't listening. He was out of his mind.

"Shhhhh," she said, rushing to him. All she could reach was his head, and there was every chance in the world she was about to get shredded by his teeth, but she couldn't stay away if she tried. "Shhhh, Kade. I'm here. I'm here."

His eyes rolled in his head as he struggled. She glanced at his body, gasped, and then closed her eyes tight. Nothing could survive that...right? *Stop it.* Gritting her teeth, she knelt down beside him and forced her hand onto the side of his face. "Kade. You're mine, do you hear me? You're mine, and I'm telling you it's not time yet. You can't leave. You won't. You're a beast, and beasts don't quit fighting. You owe me. You owe me!" When she gripped the scruff of fur at the side of his face, he snarled and twitched to the side as if he would bite her, but then his eyes locked onto hers and he froze.

"It's me," she whispered. "You aren't alone. I'm here. I won't let anything happen to you. We'll be a team, okay? You fight, and I'll fight, and when you wake up, I'll be here. I'll always be here when you wake up. Okay?"

Kade's panting sounded so pained, but he held her gaze, and he didn't bite her. Chest heaving, eyes rimmed with tears, Trina leaned forward and dared a kiss to the side of his muzzle and then nuzzled against him. "You're mine and I'm yours."

That's when she felt it. The softest touch of his tongue against her cheek. He'd licked her. She eased back and brushed her fingertips over the cheek that tingled from the wolf-kiss, but Kade's eyes were closed again.

"What the fuck was that?" Rike asked in the most shocked tone she'd ever heard from a man. "He didn't even rip your face off."

"He...he licked me," she murmured, fingers still on her cheek.

"Holy fuckin' shit, Trin," Kurt said. "Did you tame the monster?"

Heat rushed up her neck and landed in her face.

She was probably the color of a beet, and she couldn't help her dumb smile. This shouldn't be a happy moment, but Kade's wolf had really licked her instead of killing her. Trina looked down at her body in shock. She wasn't bleeding. "I thought that was going to go way different," she admitted as Ethan started stitching up the holes in Kade's shoulder.

"Uh, we all did," Rike muttered. "This wolf is a psycho. Or…he was." Rike's dark eyebrows drew down with confusion. "Trina, I think you might be a witch."

She huffed an exhausted laugh and sat down hard right by the bed, resting her hand on Kade's face, leaning her cheek on the side of the mattress. "I wish. I would make a magic potion to take his pain and put it in me."

The boys got quiet, and when she looked up, they were staring down at her with unreadable expressions. "What?" she asked.

It was Ethan who answered. "You really found him, Trina."

"Who?"

Ethan went back to work with the smallest smile on his lips, barely even visible through his beard.

"You found the one."

SIXTEEN

Fuuuuuuuuuuuuuuuuck, everything hurt.

"And so when I went in to sign the paperwork, it was this bittersweet moment..." Someone was talking in a soft murmur he could barely make out. He tried to bring his hand up to rub his forehead, but he couldn't make his arms work.

"The Darby Clan used to be in that bar almost every day..."

His head was pounding and it felt like someone had taken a sledgehammer to his body.

"I bought it with my dad, I felt really brave because I knew I would have to be in that place every day where my friends used to hang out..."

Wait, what? What was that? A TV playing?

Something brushed his face, but he was too groggy to move.

"But in a way, it was me paying tribute to the Clan after they died. They weren't always bad. In the beginning, they were good. Good for mountain lions at least, but mountain lion Clans don't have a long survival rate. The culture is to fight everything, no matter what. It's to start shit, no matter what. It's to kill everything in our territory, and when the males started coming into their own, figuring out their dominance, they started making bad decisions. Decisions that got people hurt. Not just themselves, but innocent people. Humans. Women. My dad and I backed off to the edge of the Clan and stopped going to meetings. All they did there was fuel rage and war..."

Another brush against his face. He winced. What was that? It tickled a little.

"I watch the Wulfe Clan, and they're so similar to the Old Darby Clan. They're just getting worse..."

Brush.

Kade smelled Trina's shampoo. Her favorite flavor was mango, so her hair always smelled like it. Relief washed through him. Trina was okay. She was right here beside him where he could keep her safe. He just needed to remember how to use his damn fingers again so he could stroke her hair like she was stroking his face. Kade eased his eyes open and came nose to hair with Trina. She was leaned against his bed, her head right beside him, relaxed as she talked and petted him.

Petted him.

Kade tried to frown but his face didn't work right. What the fuck? He forced air past his vocal cords, but a soft whine came out. What the fuck, what the actual fuck? He was a wolf? He was a wolf, but Trina was right here and he could hurt her. Trina! "Trin," he growled in his wolf voice he hated so much. "Run."

Trina gasped and then looked right at him, hope endless in her pretty green eyes. "Kade?" When he didn't respond because he couldn't, she repeated louder, "Kade?"

She tugged at his ears and hugged his neck. *Please don't hurt her, please don't hurt her* he begged the wolf over and over, but the wolf was quiet as he whispered in his mind, "*I would never hurt her. She's ours.*" The last word drew out, and the voice in his head faded away.

Kade laid there panting, waiting for the wolf to come back with a "just kidding" and attack Trina, but he didn't. He just sat there inside him, watching her eyes fill up with tears.

"You love me," he growled.

She ran her hand over his face over and over. "I love you very much."

"Ride or die," he huffed on a breath.

"Always. We're a team, you and me." She gripped the fur on his cheeks and rested her forehead against his. "Don't do that to me ever again. You scared me."

He'd never been so present in this form before. So aware. So in control.

He didn't even want to think about Changing, but he had to know if he could. Had to. Before Kade could change his mind, he closed his eyes and imploded. He pushed the Change as fast and as hard as he could, gritting his teeth against the agony. His snarl of pain turned into a grunt, and then he clutched the comforter in his closed fists, his body shaking for a minute before he could think straight again. He was drenched in sweat, exhausted, his bandages shredded, and his shoulder smelled like blood again.

"Why are you smiling like that?" Ethan asked

from the open doorway where he, Rike, Leah, and Bailey were piled.

Trina had backed away from him a few feet, but she was grinning, too. "Because he Changed on purpose."

Ethan and Rike exchanged glances. They looked surprised. They looked…proud. Ethan asked, "You good, man?"

"Yeah." He nodded, his eyes on Trina. "I'm good."

"Okay," Rike murmured, lingering as the others made their way back into the hallway. "Well…" He cleared his throat and looked down at the floor, scuffed it with the toe of his riding boot. "I'm really glad you didn't croak." Rike slammed the door behind him and could be heard stomping down the hallway behind the others.

What was this feeling? Belonging?

"You got good people, Kade," Trina murmured. God, she looked pretty in his Harley shirt and those little cutoff shorts. No shoes, just long fair legs curled up under her.

With a grunt, Kade pushed himself up and sat on the edge of the bed, gripping the mattress. "My insides feel like hamburger."

"Well, you got shot, ran around the woods for a while, and tried to fight me. Then you almost died while Ethan and Hairpin Trigger dug metal out of your body."

"Trigger was here?"

"Yeah, I'm guessing Kurt called him in because a grizzly is about the only thing that stands a chance against you when you're pissed. When I was a kid, my dad told me something I'll never forget. It's played in my mind every time I liked a boy. It plays in my mind now."

"What did he say?"

"He told me 'Trina, whatever you do, don't pick a weak man.' And that defined me for a long time. It defined my relationships. I ended relationships at the first sign they couldn't handle me, my life, or the animal inside me. And then along came you—big badass wolf." She shook her head slowly. "There's nothing weak about you."

Kade huffed a laugh and dropped his gaze to the floorboards. "Woman, I'm bleeding everywhere, I can barely move, and I feel like I've been hit by a fuckin' semi. There's nothing strong about me at the moment."

"Wrong. You shouldn't be alive, but here you are crackin' jokes and controlling a side of you that's ruled your entire life."

"Says the girl who chose a werewolf. Says the girl who survived countless broken bonds. Says the girl who lost her mom, controlled a mountain lion since birth, and never once acted like the victim of circumstance. Says the girl who won't quit on a man who doesn't deserve her devotion. You're fearless. Strongest woman I've ever met."

She canted her head, rocked upward, then stood and padded silently over to him. Gently, she climbed on his lap and squeezed her knees around his hips, slid her arms around his neck, her touch as soft as a breeze.

"I have a theory."

He gripped her hips and rocked her against him. "Tell me your theory."

"I think I went through all of that so I could be built into the exact right shape to match your rough edges. I think I had to go through all of that to make me strong for you."

Kade smiled. "Then I went through a lifetime of insanity to be strong enough to match you someday."

"You never stopped trying, did you, Kade?"

He gripped her hips and rocked her against his hardening dick and shook his head. "Not even for a day."

"Strong mate," she whispered, brushing her finger down his cheek.

Felt good. Felt so fuckin' good. He leaned into her touch, kissed her wrist, then latched his teeth onto it. Someday he was going to cut her hand, and ask her to cut his in return. Someday, when he knew he could be steady, after he took care of the threats from the Wulfe Clan. After he made sure she was safe from the world and from him, he was going to claim her. In his head, he already had, but she deserved the ceremony.

Trina Luna Chapman. His best friend, his obsession, his mate, his prey, his lady. She was brave enough to pick a monster and stick right there beside him no matter what. Even if it hurt her. Even if she'd been burned before, and that was the bravest thing—to give your heart to someone after being demolished.

She'd given him the gift of herself. She was medicine when he'd lived his entire life thinking there was no balm for the evil inside of him. He was changed from the inside out because she'd believed in him. She'd picked him and waited patiently while he rose up and fixed the shit that was hurting her. She'd never once made him feel bad for the wolf. She'd pointed at him and said, "Even if this is as good as you get, I accept you." And she made it his choice to stay stagnant or rise up and deserve her love. To become a better man for her.

She deserved safety.

She deserved fealty.

Protection.

Devotion.

To know that she was loved.

Trina deserved the world.

And he was going to work for the rest of his life to give it to her.

SEVENTEEN

She really should let him have his space and recover, but Trina had been so scared at the thought of never touching him again or hugging him again that she couldn't peel herself off him to save her life. So here she sat, straddling his lap, redoing the bandages he'd ripped off during his Change.

His fingers digging into her hips, pulling her closer, said he didn't want her to go either.

The fight wasn't over. War was coming, and she was scared because she'd done this before and knew how bad things could get. But for now, right now, they were okay. That wolf inside of Kade had saved him, and she loved his animal side more for it. Out in the living room, she could hear a football game on, and their friends and family in there cheering and bullshitting each other. They were safe in Kade's room. He was okay. For tonight, they could just be. Just breathe and smile and touch.

Kade's dick was swelling between her legs as she rolled her hips against him, and just for fun, she kissed him, nipping his lips because that always got him worked up. Kade groaned into her mouth as he pushed his tongue past her lips. She felt so good, he rammed into her faster, a short jerky rhythm that had his dick begging for release.

"Take your shorts off," he murmured in her ear before he sucked on her lobe.

She gasped in response, meeting his pelvic thrusts. "But Kade, you're half-dead."

"My dick is zero percent dead, woman. Stick it in. I need to feel you."

"Compromise," she whispered, dismounting him and sliding her shorts and panties down to her ankles. "I'll rub on you, and you stay still so you don't get hurt worse."

"I don't feel a fuckin' thing right now— Ooooooooow," he groaned as she pulled his Harley T-shirt over her head.

"Promise me," she said.

"Anything you want, just come sit on me." The way he said it while staring at her tits meant he didn't even know what he was agreeing to.

Well, hopefully he didn't die while they were fooling around. That would be an uncomfortable conversation to have with his family.

"Easy," she murmured, dropping to her knees in between his legs.

"You mean you want this gentle," he said, his silver eyes zeroed in on her boobs still.

"It's the only chance I have at gentle with you," she said. And then she bit her bottom lip and smiled up at him as she ran her nails up his shins and thighs. Kade's eyes rolled back in his head, and he whispered, "Fuck, Trina, put it in your mouth."

She was already purring. God, she loved when he told her what he liked, told her what to do. She cupped his balls first and listened to the sigh of ecstasy as he spread his knees wider. And then she gripped the base of his shaft and slid her mouth over him. His groan filled her belly with warmth. She loved how noisy he was. If she did something he liked, he always let her know. So sexy. She sucked on him, sliding up and down his stone-hard dick, only pausing when he rocked with her pace. Easy.

"God, it's torture," he murmured breathily. "Feels so good."

His breath hitched when she started up again, and he rested his hand behind her head and then gripped her hair. Trina reached between her legs and slid a finger inside herself. She was so ready for him. His breathing quickened as she sucked him faster, using her hand to help stroke him each time she eased back.

"Spread your legs wider, let me see," he gritted out.

Trina spread her knees wider on the floor and moved against her hand as she slid her mouth up and down his shaft. He was so thick, so hard, she wanted him inside her. She could finish so fast on him right now.

"Come here," he demanded, as if he could read her desperate thoughts.

"Easy," she pleaded as she crawled on his lap. "Let me."

She rubbed against the swollen head of his cock a few times and then reached between them, gripped his dick, and poised him right at her entrance. Slowly she eased down an inch, then up, grinning as she teased him. As she teased herself.

"Take it," he whispered in a shaky breath.

Trina lowered down, down, until she took all of him. She wiggled gently against his pelvis as he whispered, "Fuuuuuuuck."

One full stroke, and the pressure was already building between her legs. Slowly, she lifted up and then pushed back down hard. Up slow, down hard. Faster now as he gripped her hip with one hand and uttered her name. Up slow, down hard. Up, down, so easy to slide onto him when she was this wet. Kade was so big he filled her, stretched her. Reaching behind her, she cupped his balls, and his dick clenched as he moaned a sound of pure satisfaction.

"Faster," he said.

She went a little faster.

"Faster, Trina, I'm there. Come with me. Fuck, come with me!"

Trina was there too, her body tingling with desire. She slid onto him harder and faster, panting out his name until he groaned loud against her ear. His dick pulsed deep, deep inside of her, spurring on her own release. She cried out and buried her face in his neck as her body shattered. On and on, he throbbed inside of her as he held her close. "Good girl," he murmured against her ear. "That's a good girl."

She moved on him until every last aftershock was done for them both.

Today she'd thought she would never have this moment with him again, but she did because he was strong enough.

For the rest of her life, she would never take a single moment with him for granted.

****

"What happened to the wolf?" Kade asked. "Mick?"

The water sloshed as he moved his leg to a more comfortable position. Trina had drawn him a warm bath to clean off all the mud and filth from the day. He was keeping the bandages dry, but the rest of him was submerged and relaxing, muscle by fatigued muscle.

Trina was resting her chin on her arm on the edge of the bathtub, drawing little circles on the surface of the water with her free hand. "I was thinking. I don't really want to be away from you anymore at night."

Kade snorted. "You want me to hang out at the bar every night while you work? That's tempting fate. You know I'll be in a fight every night if I do that."

"No, not while I work. I mean sleeping."

"Trina."

"Hmmm?" she asked dreamily.

"What happened to Mick?"

She chewed on the side of her lip and moved her damp hair out of her face. She'd showered while he'd soaked. "How do you have a perfect eight-pack when you are relaxing in a tub. It's pretty unfair to all the other mere mortal men—"

Kade winced as he cupped her cheek. "Hey. It's me. Talk to me."

"I thought it was you. That dead wolf. Leah couldn't tell if it was you or not when she called me, and I rode here thinking I had already lost you. Red Dead Mayhem played cleaner for Mick's body. I don't know what they did with him, and I don't care."

"Okay." He stroked the pad of his thumb across her cheek, right under her flaming green eyes. She looked upset, and it gutted him. "I'm all right."

She nodded for a long time, but she was staring at the water, not him, so he hooked a finger under her chin. "Baby," he whispered, "I swear I'm all right."

"I'm really glad you're a shifter," she squeaked out.

He laughed. "I think you're the first one to ever say that to me."

She laughed thickly, too. "Well, it's true. If your wolf wasn't such a stubborn beast, you wouldn't be here." She sucked in air and admitted, "I declared war on the Wulfe Clan."

"Hmm. That's cool. I declare war on them at least twice a week."

"No…I mean I officially declared war."

"What?" Kade sat up in the bathtub, ignoring the pain. "You talked to Darius?"

"Yep, three days, and I'm squaring off with him and his Clan of emotionally devoid hairy bunions."

"Good God, Woman."

Trina lifted her little chin in the air and straightened her spine. "Now ask me if I regret it."

"Oh, I know you don't, you little hellion." Kade huffed a laugh. "Dream girl. Look!" He pointed to his dick. "You've awoken the sleeping giant again."

Trina cracked up and rested back onto her arm. "Of course, you would think starting a war is sexy."

"Nah," he said softly. "Anything you do is sexy. Tell me why you started it."

"Because they went after you. You're mine. I protect what's mine."

"You hate fighting."

"I do not," she murmured as she went back to drawing pictures on the water. Hearts this time. "Not if it's for good reason."

"Vengeance is good reason?"

"When it has to do with you, yes." When she lifted those emerald green eyes to his, the smile had disappeared from her face. There was no humor in her face at all when she said, "I would do awful things to keep you safe."

"So would I," he said low.

"I know."

"No…you don't. And hopefully you never have to find out how far I would go to keep you safe. Hopefully, I don't ever get pushed into defending you. No one would survive."

He brushed his fingertips across the gooseflesh that had risen on her arm. His touch trailed water, and the drops raced down her arm and dripped back into the bath. "Does that scare you?"

"No."

"Then why the chills?"

She intertwined her fingers in his and sighed, and there it was. There was that heart-stopping smile again. "Because all my life I thought I would never find someone like you."

Kade drew her knuckles to his lips and lingered there for a few moments. "You'll never be alone now."

Never again. He would make sure of it.

EIGHTEEN

Kade woke up in the dark to his shoulder throbbing. He'd had trouble sleeping all night, trying to find a comfortable position. Trina didn't want to leave his side, so it was both of them in a full-sized bed and him trying not to wake her with his movements. He'd taken a pain killer Rike had put on the night stand. He didn't even want to know what pharmacy he probably robbed to get it. It was a brand-new bottle of the good stuff. Knowing Rike, he'd probably enjoyed stealing this. Or maybe he just had an extra bottle of it lying around from a backache. But probably not. The Blackwood crows were and always would be outlaws. Secretly, he fucking loved them.

Kade stared up at the ceiling in the early morning light that filtered through the window. When he looked over at Trina, he was stunned all over again. Not a stitch of make-up on, and she still stole his breath away. Blond hair fanned out across his pillow, lips slightly parted, tiny frown furrowing her perfectly arched eyebrows. Dark eyelashes that rested on her cheeks, and the cutest little pixie nose.

God, he loved her. Everything about her. She was so different from anyone he'd ever known. He still couldn't believe she'd picked him. He was the luckiest sonofabitch on the whole planet.

His shoulder had a heartbeat. The pain meds had probably worn off. He gritted his teeth and sat up gingerly. No new blood on the bandages so that was good. One-handed, Kade scrubbed his hand down his face. Two more days. He needed to rush this healing so he could be there for the Wulfe Clan war. No way in hell was he going to let Trina and his brothers fight without him.

Thankfully, being a monster had its benefits. Like he healed faster than any other shifter he knew. And shifters already healed fast. He shrugged his arm up and down, testing it. No broken bones that he could tell. He was a little black and blue, but he'd be all right. No pain meds necessary anymore. He didn't like the way they made him feel. They dulled his senses.

And he needed all pistons firing to keep his ears on the wolves that were watching the house from the woods. He heard two of them all night, sniffing around. Wulfe Clan spies probably, but why did they need eyes on the house? The date and time had been set for the fight. Something was happening, and the thing about wolves was this—they didn't hunt like other predators. They came at prey unexpectedly and from all sides. Trying to guess what a wolf would do was pointless. He didn't like the wolves in the woods, but he was in no shape to go hunt those dick-wads down.

His phone was across the room on a charger, but Trina's was right there on the little table beside his bed. She probably had an alarm set for work today. He would be going with her just to make sure she was safe. He picked it up and checked the time. Five fifteen in the morning. Damn, it was early. An image flashed across the screen, but he wasn't about looking at his girl's messages so he set the phone down and stood. And then he frowned at the wall because that flash of image was burned into his mind now. It was a man in a blindfold. A familiar man.

A sick feeling drifted through him like poisonous fog. He sat on the edge of the bed and lifted the phone, opened the image, and muttered a curse.

It was Cooper, Trina's dad, hog tied, blindfolded, and gagged.

There was a long-ass text message from Darius.

I told you, bitch. You don't know who the fuck you're talking to. You'll bring Kade to me in exchange for your father. There will be no war, just an even trade. He's a wolf in my territory, with no permission from my Clan to even exist here. And now he's bested my Second. I own him. Noon at the Wulfe Clubhouse. One minute late, and Cooper dies. If you show anyone this message, Cooper dies. If you bring anyone with you other than that fuckin' wolf, Cooper dies. Involve the police, Cooper dies. You a daddy's girl, Trina? I had a step-daughter once. Treacherous little beasts, you are. But I think you have a heart for this one. I won't make it pretty. His death will be with a blade, and it'll be slow. And either way, I'll get my wolf. Do the right thing. See you soon.

Clenching his teeth, Kade set the phone back down as gently as he could because, right now, he felt like chucking it against the wall just to hear the satisfying shatter.

Barely in control of his breathing, Kade glanced at Trina. She stretched her legs in her sleep, restless, probably because he was filling the room up with his rage. *You a daddy's girl, Trina?* Fuck Darius for threatening the only family she had left. Trina was Kade's to protect, and her people fell under his umbrella of protection, too. He'd seen Cooper's black eye. Seen the rage twisting his face behind the blindfold.

Fuck!

Kade stood, made his way to the chair in the corner, and grabbed his darkest jeans and a black T-shirt that would hide any blood from his shoulder. He scribbled a quick note to Trina on a piece of computer paper, folded it, and left it on the bedside table. And then made his way out the door. He checked Trina just before he closed it. Sleeping soundly again. Angel.

He needed to do this quickly before she woke up. Yeah, they were a team, but things were different when family was at risk. Kade had an awful flashback of his dad hurt on the couch after that bad fight, and how every fiber of his being had wanted to help him no matter what. Trina wouldn't think straight in a fight like this.

He had to fix it, and fast.

The house was dark except the kitchen where Ethan was making a bowl of oatmeal. "Where are you going?" he asked without turning around.

"None of your business."

His back to Kade, Ethan poured honey into his breakfast and stirred it around. He was already dressed for the day.

"Everyone still asleep?" Kade asked nonchalantly as he pulled his boots on by the door.

"The girls are."

He glared at his back suspiciously. He was wearing black jeans and a black Harley shirt. Outside, it was still dark. "Why are you dressed?"

Ethan turned and brought two bowls straight for Kade and handed him one.

"What's this?"

"Breakfast. Momma Crow brought some medicine that's supposed to speed your healing. It's for shifters only. Black market stuff. You're welcome."

Kade sniffed the bowl of oatmeal. "Smells like shrimp shit."

"Bon appétit." Ethan clinked spoons with Kade's. Annoying.

"I'm not eating this. It'll put me to sleep."

Ethan rolled his eyes before he took a big spoonful of Kade's breakfast and then shoved it in his maw. He pulled a face as he chewed it. "It's not a sleeping potion, ya dunce. It's to help you fight today."

Kade narrowed his eyes. "The war isn't for another two days," he said carefully.

Ethan snorted. "You're a Blackwood—"

"Not technically—"

"You're Blackwood enough," Ethan said, his eyes flashing black. "You're family. Me and Rike talked last night, and if it was us, we would want immediate retaliation. We wouldn't draw this out. We would go in early."

Kade huffed. "Well, you aren't me." He choked down the breakfast in three bites, then finished tying his shoes.

When he made his way to the back door, Ethan

stopped him in his tracks. "If you're worried about going out the front because of the wolves watching the house? You don't have to be."

Kade looked back over his shoulder. Ethan's eyes were black as pitch.

"Why not?" Kade asked.

"Because Rike locked them up in the woodshop. The woods are clear."

Huh. Clever crows.

"Well...thanks," Kade muttered, making his way quietly to the front door. "Tell Trina not to worry when she wakes up."

"No, thanks," Ethan said, following him right out the front.

Kade threw him a dirty look. "What are you doing?"

"Uh, going with you." He jerked his chin in a greeting and threw up a two fingered wave to Rike who was jogging toward them.

"You're not going with me, Ethan. Neither of you are. This is Lone Wolf shit. It's my fight with the Wulfe Clan, no one else's."

Ethan kept following him, so Kade snarled and shoved him in the shoulder. Should've hurt Kade more than anything, but whatever medicine Momma Crow had sent over was dulling the pain in his shoulder by the minute.

"Go away," Kade muttered.

Ethan stood there with his hands on his hips, grinning through his giant-ass beard. Kade wanted to punch him.

"My fight, my retaliation, piss off."

"I know you're used to this Lone Wolf shit, but I'm not staying in that house," Ethan said. "That hellcat you call a mate will skin me alive if she finds out I just let you walk out of here to fight the Wulfe Clan alone. Mountain lion in heat, and I'm about to get her favorite dick snuffed out of existence? No, thanks. It's brotherly bonding time."

"Murdering a Clan isn't brotherly bonding time."

"It is to Blackwoods. You heard the story about our dad? It's kind of our destiny to kill off the wolves. No offense to your wolf."

What the hell was happening right now? This wasn't how this was supposed to go. "I was going to sneak out, go on a small to medium killing-spree, save Trina's dad, and be back by lunch for roast beef sandwiches and an epic blow job for *saving her dad*!"

"I'll drive," Rike offered, tossing an apple in the air and catching it as he approached. He looked like a damn goliath in his black tank top, tattoos on display on his tree-trunk arms.

"I'm not riding bitch on your motorcycle, man. That means putting my nuts on your back. I would rather stick my dick in a mouse trap," Kade whisper-screamed, following his stepbrother toward where the bikes were parked.

"We're taking the truck, numbnuts," Rike said. "Bikes are too loud, and we won't get to murder anyone if you get us busted before we even get there."

"You drive like shit. I'm driving. Give me the keys," Ethan demanded.

Rike snorted. "You aren't the Alpha of me."

"It's my mate's truck," Ethan retorted, shoving Rike hard into the back end of Leah's old Ford. He blasted into it so hard the thing lifted on two wheels and settled hard.

"Shhhh!" Kade hissed. "For fuck's sake, tweedled dee and tweedled dip-shit. This is why I wanted to do this on my own."

"You're not going on a killing spree without us!"

Rike hissed back. "I fuckin' hate Bailey's dad, and you're gonna off him without me to witness? I don't think so. It's not just your retaliation! And I haven't murdered anyone in a long time!"

"Me either," Ethan said, yanking open the driver's side door. "And Rike is tweedle dip-shit. You pointed at me when you said that, but you should've pointed at him."

All those years following Rike and Ethan, and Kade had been so wrong. Having brothers was the worst.

The front door creaked open loudly. "Kade?" Trina called from the house.

All three of them froze. The apple Rike had just tossed in the air hit the ground and rolled into Kade's boot. Ethan had one leg hiked up into the truck already, and Kade was thinking of ten ways to kill the Blackwood Idiots.

Kade narrowed his eyes at Ethan and mouthed, *Mother fucking fucker.*

He wanted to rip that stupid smile off Ethan's face as he formed the words, *Oops.*

Great. Now there was double hell to pay.

NINETEEN

"What's going on?" Trina asked as she padded through the yard barefoot.

"Uuuuh," Kade said, turning around slowly. "We were going to get you girls some donuts?"

"Bullshit." She held up the note he'd written her. "You wrote me a note that says, and I quote, 'Even when I'm not here, I'll always love you.' You never write mushy stuff like that, and some trip to the donut store isn't going to get you to write a goodbye letter to me. That's what this is, right? A goodbye letter for just-in-case? And you drew a heart by my name. A heart! And why the hell would all three of you be dressed like Johnny Cash to go get some donuts?"

"What's happening?" Leah asked sleepily from the house.

"Where are you guys going?" Bailey asked from beside Leah.

Fury blasted through Trina as it all started making sense. She stomped her foot. "I'll tell you where they're going. They're going to fight your dad, Bailey!"

Bailey yawned loudly. "Darius isn't my dad. Not anymore. He's an asshole and probably better off dead."

Trina glanced behind her to see if Bailey was serious, but yep, she was leaned against the banister, white hair and pale skin practically glowing like a ghost as she chewed on her thumbnail.

"Well, I want to go," Leah said. "Are we still getting donuts, though?"

Ethan was chuckling now, Trina was feeling very strongly about Kade marching off to war injured, it was way too early in the morning, the goodbye letter had scared her, and she was feeling eighty-three percent dramatic right about now. "This isn't funny! Kade is on his death bed!"

"Actually, I feel totally fine," Kade said with a

shrug.

He wore a crooked smile, and he hadn't shaved. His muscular arms were stretching the thin fabric of his black V-neck T-shirt, and why did he have to be annoying and hot at the same time? Her brain was mad, but her ovaries were panting like overheated chihuahuas.

"What do you mean you're totally fine?" Trina asked, stomping her way right up to him. "You were groaning all night."

Leah stopped beside her and murmured, "That's what she said."

Now Bailey and Rike were laughing, and this was too much.

Kade cracked a smile and then cleared his throat as though trying to cover it. "Momma Crow gave me some drugs, and now I feel fine. To…you know…go get some donuts."

Trina blinked slowly and counted to three, praying for patience. "Okay. Go on then." She put her hands up in the air and backed away a few steps. "Have fun. Bring me back a chocolate-covered donut with sprinkles."

Kade narrowed his eyes to suspicious little silver

slits. "Seriously?"

"Yeah, seriously. I'm super hungry. Maybe get a half-dozen."

"She looks scary," Rike whispered. "Just go."

Suspicious-looking as hell, Kade made his way to the passenger's side of the truck with Rike, and just before he got in, he said, "We'll be back in two hours."

"I can't wait to see you again," she sang out.

"Dude," Rike said, "your mate is not a morning person."

Leah raised her hand at Ethan. "Babe, get me a glazed one and a white coconut—Ack!" she screeched as Trina dragged her by the hand to the bed of the truck.

Bailey was already lowering the tailgate like she knew exactly what Trina had in mind, and the truck engine roared to life.

"What the hell are you doing?" Ethan demanded from where he was hanging out of the driver's side open window.

After the girls scrambled into the back, Trina pulled the tailgate closed. She looked through the suicide window, daring any one of those boys to say something.

They all looked defeated, so no arguments from them. Trina crossed her arms and sat between Bailey and Leah against the cab of the truck.

As they headed up the road, Leah broke the silence. "Trina, I think this is a very bad idea."

"Why?"

Leah sighed. "Because you aren't wearing any pants."

Trina looked down at her long bare legs splayed out in the bed of the truck. Leah was right. No pants. "Well, that is unfortunate."

"Now we really can't get donuts," Bailey muttered.

Trina snorted at the ridiculousness of the last few minutes. She looked over at Bailey who was biting back a smile, too. When Leah cackled, Bailey lost it, and Trina cracked up, too. Everything was a mess. "Okay, maybe I didn't think this through, but in my defense," she punched out between her laughter, "it was a very long day and a very long night and I haven't had my coffee and I got mad at Kade and the boys and…and…"

"You turned into a wrecking ball?" Bailey asked.

"Yes. But I really love how you two crawled right

in the back of the truck with me."

"I didn't," Leah piped up between giggling. "You dragged me in here. I wanted to go back to bed. Clearly, one of us is a better friend than the other." She pointed her finger at Bailey.

The window slid open right behind Trina's head, and Kade's hand rested onto her shoulder comfortingly. "I'm sorry," he murmured.

With a sigh, Trina laid her cheek against his warm hand, holding it tight.

Through the window, Kade told her, "Darius has your dad."

Those four words...she couldn't make sense of them.

Darius.

Has.

Your.

Dad.

She just sat there, frozen like some stone statue, staring out at the road behind them illuminated by the taillights.

"I was gonna bring him back to you before you woke up," he murmured.

"Is he okay?" she squeaked out.

"They won't hurt him," Bailey murmured. "It's just one of their plays. They're weak. They've been making decisions that have crippled them little by little. Dad—Darius—he's not a good Alpha anymore. He hasn't been for a while. But if they have Cooper, and they're letting you know? It means he's the only chess piece they have in position."

Bailey frowned and sniffed the air. "It also means he's a diversion. Look." She pointed into the dark woods. A set of glowing eyes stared back at them.

The truck sputtered, coughed, and eased to a stop.

A single howl pierced the air, and Bailey whispered, "Oh, shit."

Ethan tried the engine again, but the truck was barely responding. Rike and Kade got out, rushed to the front and popped the hood.

"It has to be the gas line, right?" Kade asked.

"Feels like it," Rike answered.

"Look," Leah said low from where she was standing in the bed, staring out over the top of the truck. She was pointing to something on the road ahead.

Trina scrambled up beside her, heart pounding

out of her chest.

Just on the edge of the headlight beams, two more sets of glowing eyes appeared.

"Kaaaade," she warned.

"I hear them," her mate said solemnly. "Fuck. I bet they cut a notch in all the gas lines in the motorcycles, too. They just needed us to get out here in the middle of nowhere for an ambush. Fuckin' wolves." His voice was a snarl by the end, and he slammed the hood of the truck down.

"How many do they have?" Trina asked Bailey as the she-wolf jumped out of the bed of the truck with a snarl in her throat.

She muttered off names. "Mick's dead, so eight left if Darius's shit ideas haven't run more of the Clan off. Picking a fight with the goddamn Blackwoods. Lost his mind."

"There's two wolves tied up in the woodshop," Trina said. Why was she shaking? Oh, right. Because she'd been in a shifter war before, and her entire damn Clan got themselves killed.

"Then six, but look," Kade said, coming to stand beside Trina. The woods were alive with glowing eyes now. "There's way more than six wolves hunting us."

"They must've called in more wolf Clans to boost their numbers," Bailey murmured in an inhuman voice. "Maybe the Kill Jumpers and the Hell Bringer Clans. They both owe the Wulfe Clan blood favors." Her eyes were glowing like the ones in the woods. Kade's, too, and Leah's.

"Hey, Ramsey," Ethan said into his phone. "The Wulfe Clan has Cooper up at their clubhouse. How fast can you—"

A huge brown wolf slammed into Ethan, and they crashed against the side of the truck so hard the back end skidded to the side.

A white wolf exploded out of Bailey, and Leah pitched forward and fell to all fours before a black wolf tore out of her. Ethan threw the wolf into a tree, but the others were coming now.

"My phone," Ethan said, searching frantically.

But there wasn't time to search the dark woods for where it had landed because Ethan and Rike took the full force of three wolves just as they stepped out of the glow of the headlights.

Trina closed her eyes and searched for the mountain lion. She just felt empty, though. There was nothing there. No power, no teeth, no claws, no snarl in her throat... She felt...human.

"Trina, Change!" Kade said, standing between her and two approaching wolves. Bailey and Leah were already in snarling, violent fights of their own. She could barely see them in the dark. Only hear them and see a flash of white fur every second or so.

Lion, where are you? The bullet that had ripped through Kade was sitting in her pocket in his room. She imagined it, imagined holding the bloody thing that had almost taken her mate's life. But still...no mountain lion.

"Kade," she said, panicking. "I can't Change."

"Baby, you have to," he murmured, backing her up against the truck as the two mottled black and brown wolves approached, their heads lowered, muzzles wrinkled, gold eyes glowing, teeth gnashing as they growled. "Right now. There's no more time."

"I don't have the lion!"

When Kade glanced over his shoulder for just a split second, his eyes were bone-white. His face was twisted with rage and looked different, looked terrifying, as if he'd already begun his Change. Half man, half monster. Her monster.

"There's a shotgun under the seat."

Kade tensed and dove for the wolves. And right before he hit them, his own gray wolf ripped out of him.

And for a moment, Trina was awed into stillness. He latched onto one wolf's neck and jerked his head back and forth with such power the thing yelped and went limp in his jaws. The other wolf was attacking his back, but if Kade felt it, he showed no signs of pain. He spun and latched onto the wolf's front leg. *Snap.*

Three more sets of eyes were running at them fast from the woods.

She'd never been so terrified. She had no weapons. No way to protect herself, no way to protect her friends. No way to help her mate.

"Rike, get help!" Ethan yelled from under two wolves, and with a series of pops, Rike and Ethan Changed into their crows and took to the skies. The crow with a noose of white feathers around its neck returned, diving for the wolves, but the pure black one flew away and didn't come back. God speed to the crow, because they were grossly outnumbered out here and unprepared. The woods were deafening with the sounds of a snarling, growling, ripping war.

There's a shotgun under the seat. "Okay," she whispered, bolting the three steps to the door. She reached for the handle and yanked it open, but it slammed shut again as a wolf blasted against it. The thing landed on the ground and jumped at her, latched onto her arm the second she went to defend her face.

And God, did it hurt.

Lion!

The wolf wouldn't release her, shaking its head with such force she could feel the teeth grinding against her wrist bones. The wolf leaned its weight back, and Trina got pulled forward. If she toppled, her throat and belly would be vulnerable. Gritting her teeth against the pain, she splayed her feet and grabbed the scruff of the wolf's neck to ease the tension on her arm, and then she slammed it into the truck as hard as her shifter strength would allow. She wasn't weaponless, she realized. Not totally. She had strength and agility. So when the wolf hit the metal of the truck and released her arm, she was already moving for the door. The damn door was damaged though, dented inward and didn't open when she tried the handle, so she dropped down in desperation and slid under the truck. She could hear the snarling wolf behind her, but it was big and had trouble getting under the truck, so she army crawled to the other side, swallowing down her fear at the breath she felt on her ankles and the snapping of teeth so close. It was all she could hear. Grunting, she pulled herself up and yanked open the driver's side door as fast as she could, scrambled in, and screamed as she closed it on the muzzle of the wolf.

With shaking hands, she reached under the seat. The bed of the truck groaned as something jumped into the back. Wolves were howling in the distance. Too many of them. The truck was lurching to and fro from battles hitting the sides. Panting, Trina glanced over her shoulder and swallowed a scream. A massive black wolf was right there, lips pulled back over bloody teeth. Why were his teeth bloody? "Kade!" she screamed.

The suicide window was open, and the Wolf had shoved his head through as far as he could, gnashing his teeth, scrabbling to get to her. She pinned herself to the steering wheel, her back against the horn. *Beeeeeeeep!* It sounded long and high, right along

with the howling wolves. The teeth were so close.
God, don't let that window break!

She stretched her arm as far under the seat as she could. "Come on, come on, come on!"

Her fingertips touched metal just as the window made a terrifying cracking sound, like walking on a frozen pond where the ice is too thin. No, no, no.

The growling of the wolf filled the entire cab of the truck, drowning out everything, drowning out the horn and the war outside. All she could hear was the animal's death-promise.

Crack, crack, crack.

She could see the hairline fractures in the glass moving outward. It wouldn't hold much longer. Clenching her jaw, she stretched as far as she could, got as close to the wolf's snapping teeth as she dared. Got it!

Trina fell to the floor the second the wolf gave her an inch and pulled the barrel of the shotgun up. There was a box of shells under the seat, and her hands shook so bad while she rushed to crack the barrel in half and shove two shells inside. The sound of metal on metal was loud as she clicked the rifle into place and cocked it.

In that second, the glass gave, shattering all over her, and the wolf came right at her.

Click, click. Boom!

Trina closed her eyes at the deafening sound of a shotgun discharged at close range.

The wolf fell inside the cab, completely limp, gold eyes dimming as it stared back at her.

Trina was splattered with blood, and she sucked air as she slid out from under its weight. She pushed the handle of the door, opening it to escape the dead wolf, but while on her back, she looked up and saw another one coming straight for the truck, straight for the open door, straight for her, his teeth bared, ready to end her. Trina screamed in fury as she pulled the barrel of the shotgun up, aimed, and pulled the trigger. The gun kicked hard because she hadn't been able to put it against her shoulder. The wolf went down, skidding under the truck, its shoulders getting stuck right near the front tire. Trina scrambled out of the cab, yanked the box of shells across the floorboard. When she opened up the shotgun, two empty, smoking shells flipped out onto the ground. She replaced them, clicked the weapon into place, and cocked it. *Click, click.*

Dad hadn't taken her shooting for a couple years, so she had to knock the rust off a little. But with a shotgun, her aim could be a little off and still do the job. It was a forgiving weapon in a fight like this, as long as she kept her targets at close range.

Kade was fighting a cream-colored wolf. Darius? They were just shredding each other. There were wolves piled around them, but they avoided the carnage like some war dance. When another wolf came sailing through the trees, running straight for Kade, Trina aimed. *Boom!*

Click, click.

The first streaks of dawn were lightening the woods, but it was still hard to see. Even with her shifter eyesight, she had to squint to make sure she wasn't aiming at Kade or Leah. Bailey was easy. She was pure white like the snow. No other wolf looked like her. But Leah had tar-black fur and was hard to see in the dark.

Two wolves came barreling through the trees and crossed the road, headed for Bailey's fight.

Boom! Down went one, but the other changed its course and headed straight for her.

Mother trucker, she needed to reload. *Steady*

hands, do it right. She could hear the predator panting, almost to her. She reloaded one chamber—it's all she had time to do—and then she cocked it. *Click, click...click*. Shit! The wolf was on her, sailing through the air. *Click, click, boom!*

She ducked out of the way as the wolf landed right where she'd been.

Kade was fighting three wolves now. She didn't know where Leah and Bailey were. Ethan was diving at Kade's fight, but her mate was locked in a battle to the death with Darius.

Trina gasped as the edge of the woods filled with glowing eyes.

Too many.

Way too many.

They were just standing there, watching Kade war with the massive wolf. Near the truck, Leah and Bailey limped up, fur matted with crimson, heads lowered as they're eyes stayed trained on Kade's fight, too.

So many wolves.

She only had four shells left. The single empty shell smoked as it flipped from the open shotgun and fell to the ground.

And just as it touched the pine needle blanket of the forest floor, silence descended onto the woods. Trina jerked her attention to Kade, but he wasn't looking at her. Laying on his belly, he had the neck of Darius Wulfe in his teeth as he watched a black speckled wolf slink away. The Alpha didn't move. Beside Trina, Bailey leaned heavily onto the side of the truck and stared at nothing. Poor Bailey. Tough Bailey. It didn't matter if her ex-step-father was better off dead. Darius had been the only father she'd known.

There had to be thirty wolves here, watching, waiting for some signal to attack, but it didn't come.

One of the wolves lifted its nose into the air and gave a long, steady howl.

Kade released the limp Alpha. He was bigger than any wolf here, but he wasn't the Kade she'd known before. He was in control, steady, and wasn't savagely tearing through every last Clan member just to sate bloodlust. He let off an answering howl that rose and rose.

The wolves lowered their heads and stalked forward, but their paws against the dry leaves weren't the only sounds of the woods anymore.

"Caw, caw, caw, caw!"

"Caw, caw, caw!"

The flapping of wings replaced Kade's howl. When he took a breath and howled again, Trina went to stand beside him. Fog was creeping through the early morning woods, setting a haze to everything.

Every muscle in her body shook from adrenaline dumps and crashes. Her arm was drip—drip—dripping into the dry leaves as she held the lowered shotgun in front of her, aimed at the ground but ready to lift the nose the second the wolves attacked. The branches of the trees around them sagged with the weight of massive crows. Red Dead Mayhem was here. Rike had brought help. In the distance, a bear roared. It was so loud it vibrated the ground under Trina's feet. Another bear answered, and then another. A panther screamed. Kurt must be here with the Two Claws Clan.

Relief washed through her, and the gun sagged in her hands. "If you attack, you'll all die," she yelled into the woods, her words echoing. "And for what? The Alpha of the Wulfe Clan is dead. I'm tired. We're all tired. There's been enough death and bloodshed in this territory. These woods were a sanctuary, and now they'll be haunted with the ghosts of your Clans. And again...for what? So you can get revenge? So you can have more territory? So you can have the town? Every Clan here has managed to set up alliances and band together...except for the wolves. Your treachery backfired." Trina inhaled deeply and blew out a breath. "You have two options. You can leave now, leave the territory, and never come back, or you can all die."

Out of the woods behind them lumbered two enormous grizzlies, a mountain lion, and two polar bears. Two Claws were here.

The wolves were tucking their tails. "This territory belongs to us," she called out, resting her hand on Kade's back as he snarled at the intruders. "You aren't welcome in these woods. This town. This county. This is your eviction notice, assholes."

And as Kade made his way toward them, lips peeled back, the darker gray fur along his spine all spiked up, his ears flattened, and that terrifying growl she'd grown to love rattling his throat...the wolves slunk away and disappeared into the fog.

Seconds drifted by, and still, the wolves retreated. Exhaling, Trina sank down to her knees on the edge of the road. She was exhausted, and her arm hurt so bad. She clutched it to her stomach as if that would make it any better. Her skin was speckled with the blood of those wolves who had failed to kill her.

"Cooper's okay," Rike said from behind the truck. He'd Changed into his human form and was staring at a cell phone. "Ramsey sent Kasey and a couple of the guys to get him. They're bringing him back to the Red Dead Mayhem clubhouse to fix him up now, but he's fine. Already bitchin' about bein' hungry for steak and eggs."

Trina huffed a laugh. "Of course, he is."

Her friends looked bloodied and beaten, but they were still here, still upright. And Kade—her Kade—he was looking back over his shoulder with steady silver eyes that swam with pride and relief. And sanity.

They were okay.

He turned and made his way back to her, limping deeply. He searched her face, for what, she didn't know. "I'm okay," she whispered. "More than okay."

Why? Because she hadn't lost her people like she feared she would. Dad was okay, Kade was okay. Her friends who had become family were okay.

Two Claws, Red Dead Mayhem, The New Darby Clan, the Blackwood Crows. Four Clans of shifters had come together to help Kade. To help her. She'd always felt on the outside, too afraid to really give her heart to people she cared about, too afraid to lose them, but she'd stunted her life that way. Loss happened. But she owed it to herself and to Kade to have enough faith in her people to open up to them. If she hadn't done that, she wouldn't be sitting here in the middle of monsters, cupping the face of her ferocious and loving mate, absorbing the very first moment of her life when she felt she really and truly belonged.

EPILOGUE

Leah opened the door to Kade's bedroom, and smiled brightly at Trina. "Hey, little antisocial butterfly. You okay?"

Trina wiped her cheeks really fast and composed her face, then nodded. "I'm great."

Leah frowned and came to sit next to her on the bed. "You don't have to cut him, Trin."

"Oh, goodness, that's not the reason for the tears. I can't wait to belong to Kade." Her eyes were filling again, but they were happy tears. They leaked a lot lately. There had been so many changes in her life, all for the better, and all because of Kade. Like this. Leah was holding her hand, searching her face with those silver wolf-eyes, worry written all over every feature.

Kade had given her Leah. And Ethan, Rike, and...and... Trina swallowed hard and pressed her hands on her flat belly.

Big changes were still to come.

She stood, smoothed the wrinkles from her white, lacy sundress, slipped her feet into a pair of worn cowgirl boots, and grabbed the small gift bag. It bumped against her leg with every step she took toward the front of Leah's house. Every step she took toward her mate.

The sun was so bright as she stepped out onto the porch. She winced and held her hand up to shield the glare, and when she opened her eyes again, he was there, standing in the middle of their family and friends.

All four ally Clans and his parents. Barbecue and beer. That was what he'd wanted for today.

It was perfect.

He was talking to Ethan and Rike, dressed in a white Harley T-shirt that clung to the curves of his muscles just right.

Perfect.

He laughed so easy, head thrown back, eyes on Rike, bright white smile stunning her into stillness.

She breathed for that smile on him. He used to be the keeper of so few smiles, and now look at him. Happy. Healthy. All those years of fighting…of never giving up…of never fully giving into an out of control wolf, and look where he landed. Look how he ended up.

Perfect.

A flyaway lock of hair came out of her loosely pinned updo and fell into her face. As she moved to tuck it behind her ear, Kade's attention snapped right to her. The smile on his face fell slightly when he dragged his gaze down her body and back up.

Wow, he mouthed. *You look perfect.*

Her belly filled with butterflies.

Perfect.

Dad was waiting at the bottom of the stairs. He held an arm out formally. His blue eyes were rimmed with tears, and the corners were wrinkled with his emotional smile.

"Hey sweetie," he murmured.

"Hey, Dad."

He patted her hand as she slipped it in the crook of his arm.

"Dad?"

"Yeah?"

"Remember when I was a kid, and you talked about what kind of man I deserved? And you told me not to pick a weak man?"

His smile got so wide. "I remember." He jerked his head toward Kade. "And you listened. For once."

She laughed thickly and rested her forehead on his shoulder for a second before she let him take her to Kade. His mom and dad were standing near him. It was his dad who stepped forward. "Welcome to the family, Trina," he murmured, wiping his eyes behind his sunglasses. He offered her a knife. She recognized the handle. It looked like the ones Kade had gifted her those weeks ago. This time, the wolf and the mountain lion were right beside each other on the handle.

We are not separate.

Perfect.

Her dad handed Kade a matching one and shook his hand. Trina lifted her chin and looked her mate right in his striking silver eyes.

Kade shook his head slowly and stared at her like she was the moon and the stars. "I can't believe you're mine, Trina. You told me something once that changed the entire way I saw myself. You said, 'You aren't crazy.' And that faith in me made me work harder to be a man you deserved. A better man. I am a little crazy, though, Trina Luna Chapman. I'm crazy about you. You came in and turned everything I knew upside down. I was doing so much wrong before I met you, and you were the first thing I ever really got right. Pretty girl, I love you now, and I'll love you for always. You'll never have to question if you're safe because you have the protection of my body. You'll never have to question if your heart is protected because you have my soul." Kade brushed his knuckle gently across her cheek and tucked the flyaway curl behind her ear again. "I can't imagine a single moment without you, and I'm honored to be your choice."

Perfect.

Trina was trying so hard to keep it together, but there were sniffles in the crowd and Leah was losing it fairly loudly. She held out her hand, and he cut it. It hurt, but it was a sting that was temporary, and this scar, the same scar so many shifters had been giving for generations, would be a reminder of his love.

Trina blew out a steadying breath and cut his hand, linked their fingers, and then pressed her palm to his. She looked up into his eyes and said, "When I was thinking about today, I wanted to bind us in every way I could. You give me purpose. You make me feel safe and secure, and I never question if I'm loved because you are there reminding me every day. I thought a match for me didn't exist, and then you came and showed me it's okay to let people in. I asked your brothers what crows do for ceremonies like this. I know you aren't a crow, but they've called you their brother over and over the last couple months, so it feels fitting. Ethan said crows give each other gifts when they choose each other. You've been giving me gifts this whole time, probably more gifts than you even realize." She released his hand and offered him the small white gift bag.

He canted his head, and his dark brow furrowed slightly. "What's this?" he asked pulling the tissue paper out of it.

Trina pursed her lips against her overwhelming emotions as he reached for the wooden carvings in the bottom. They had little magnets on them so they were all stuck together.

We are not separate.

He dropped the empty bag and turned the

figurines in his hands. "There's three," he murmured in confusion. "Wolf...mountain lion..." Kade pulled the wolf pup from the side of the mountain lion and held it up with a questioning look.

"I don't know if our baby will be a wolf or a mountain lion, so I just took a guess. There is the reason I haven't been able to Change."

Kade's eyes went wide, and he looked back at the little family of carvings. Carefully, he placed the wolf pup back on the mountain lion, then jerked his attention to her again. His chest heaving, he dropped to his knees. "Trin, are you serious?" he asked, gripping her hips. "You gotta baby? My baby?"

She would lose it if she said a single word, so she nodded her head instead and clasped her uncut hand over her mouth as twin tears streaked down her cheeks.

He stared at her tummy and shook his head slowly back and forth, back and forth. "I never thought... I never thought I was going to be worthy of..."

"You're going to be"—her breath hitched—"*great* at this."

Kade slid his hands around her back and pulled

her tight against him, resting his ear on her stomach. As she ran her fingers through his hair, she committed this exact moment to memory.

The family that was crying happy tears for them. The friends who had shown up just to watch them bind their lives together. The little miracle in her belly. The gift Kade had given her without even realizing how important it would be for them and their future. The wolves were gone, the alliances between her friends were concrete, and this right here was the moment that changed an entire life.

This was a moment she wanted to remember for always.

Because even with the uncertainty of life as a shifter, she knew without a shadow of a doubt that she and Kade were at the very beginning of their story. And it was going to be a beautiful one.

We are not separate. From this day forward, she and Kade would never be separate again.

And everything was perfect.

Want more of these characters?

Red Dead Mayhem is a standalone series,
but the characters can first bee seen in the
bestselling Outlaw Shifters series.

For more of these characters, check out these other
books from T. S. Joyce.

For the Love of an Outlaw
(Outlaw Shifters, Book 1)

A Very Outlaw Christmas
(Outlaw Shifters, Book 2)

For the Heart of an Outlaw
(Outlaw Shifters, Book 3)

For the Heart of the Warmaker
(Outlaw Shifters, Book 4)

For the Soul of an Outlaw
(Outlaw Shifters, Book 5)

About the Author

T.S. Joyce is devoted to bringing hot shifter romances to readers. Hungry alpha males are her calling card, and the wilder the men, the more she'll make them pour their hearts out. She werebear swears there'll be no swooning heroines in her books. It takes tough-as-nails women to handle her shifters.

She lives in a tiny town, outside of a tiny city, and devotes her life to writing big stories. Foodie, wolf whisperer, ninja, thief of tiny bottles of awesome smelling hotel shampoo, nap connoisseur, movie fanatic, and zombie slayer, and most of this bio is true.

Bear Shifters? Check

Smoldering Alpha Hotness? Double Check

Sexy Scenes? Fasten up your girdles, ladies and gents, it's gonna to be a wild ride.

> For more information on T. S. Joyce's work,
> visit her website at
> www.tsjoyce.com

Printed in Great Britain
by Amazon